HITLER: THE LAST TEN DAYS

Fontana books about World War II

The Last Battle   *Cornelius Ryan*
The First and the Last   *Adolf Galland*
El Alamein   *Michael Carver*
Duce!   *Richard Collier*
Rommel   *Desmond Young*
Skis Against the Atom   *Knut Haukelid*

and many others

WARREN TUTE

Hitler:
The Last
Ten Days

Based on the original screenplay by Ennio de Concini,
Maria Pia Fusco and Wolfgang Reinhardt.

FONTANA/ Collins

First published by Fontana Books 1973

© in the novelisation, World Film Services Ltd.
and Warren Tute

Printed in Great Britain by
Love & Malcomson Ltd., Brighton Road,
Redhill, Surrey.

ILLUSTRATIONS

Hitler and Eva Braun (*Keystone Press Agency Ltd.*)

Alec Guinness plays the title role in the film, *Hitler: The Last Ten Days*

Hitler, the orator, in a characteristic pose (*Keystone Press Agency Ltd.*)

Magda and Josef Goebbels with their six children (*Keystone Press Agency Ltd.*)

On 28 April 1945, news of Himmler's offer of surrender reached Hitler (*Keystone Press Agency Ltd.*)

Hitler's pet dog, Blondi, was poisoned by his doctor (*Keystone Press Agency Ltd.*)

Eva Braun (*right*) and her sister (*Keystone Press Agency Ltd.*)

Hermann Goering was captured and committed suicide in 1946 (*Keystone Press Agency Ltd.*)

One of the few photographs of the elusive Martin Bormann (*Keystone Press Agency Ltd.*)

Hitler's 'wedding reception'; a scene from the film, *Hitler: The Last Ten Days*

ONE

Berlin, 20 April 1945. The magnificent capital of the Third Reich lay in ruins. Allied bombing from the air and artillery fire from the British, American and Russian armies as they closed in on the city had reduced its great buildings to rat-infested heaps of rubble. The two million remaining inhabitants were near to starvation. Ironically, this was the Fuehrer's birthday.

It was a spring day, with pale sunlight shining on the bomb-wrecked buildings. Three small children played beside the body of a soldier strung up on a lamp-post. There was a notice pinned to his jacket which read 'I do not believe in the Fuehrer'; an old woman pushed a pram full of firewood; a dead soldier lay at the wheel of a wrecked army truck; a pale-faced boy of the Hitler Youth, in a peaked cap and an outsize army greatcoat stood guard over a partly destroyed bridge. And past it all moved a procession of Mercedes flying the Nazi war pennant, carrying the remaining high-ranking officers and civilians to the Chancellery.

The Fuehrer was 56. Berlin might be devastated – even the façade of the vast Reichschancellery was bomb-scarred – but the SS guards who opened the car doors and presented arms, the immaculate turnout of the generals and admirals and the cool manner of important civilians and cabinet members such as Ribbentrop, Himmler, Speer and even the small limping Dr Goebbels gave scarcely any clues that the end was near.

Every senior officer who remained in Berlin arrived. Indeed, none of them could risk being absent on the Fuehrer's birthday. As each of the car doors opened and their passengers stepped out, they looked up towards the steps of the Chancellery. And as they began to climb, the metallic, assured voice of Josef Goebbels, Minister of Propaganda, richochetted from the loudspeakers on either side:

'In this dark hour of our history, it is fitting to remember that our Fuehrer is the only champion in whom we can pledge our trust. We owe it to him alone that Germany is still alive at this hour . . . history will remember the acts of our Fuehrer long after those of Julius Caesar are forgotten.'

Among the first to arrive was the Foreign Minister, Joachim von Ribbentrop. Arrogance was etched into every feature of his gaunt face. He was followed by Wilhelm Keitel, Chief of the High Command of the Armed Forces – the overall Commander-in-Chief of the German Army, Navy and Air Force. Keitel was accompanied by his second in command, Generaloberst Alfred Jodl, his face showing signs of anxiety and exhaustion.

After them it was the turn of Heinrich Himmler, Reichsfuehrer of the SS, Minister of the Interior, Chief of the State Police and of the State Secret Police, Chief of the Reich Security Service and of the Concentration Camps. He glanced to left and right, his eyes gleaming behind their round spectacles, but he gave no signal or gesture of recognition to anyone. Apart from the Fuehrer himself, no-one had played a darker or more sinister role in the previous six years.

After Himmler came Josef Goebbels, Reich Minister of Propaganda, Minister for Total War, Gauleiter of Berlin. He stopped to listen for a moment or so to the sound of his own voice – a professional checking on the effect of his work – and then he limped up the steps.

His car pulled away and was replaced by another carrying Grand Admiral Karl Doenitz, Commander-in-Chief of the German Navy and yet another, from which stepped

Dr Albert Speer, Reich Minister for Armaments – Architect in Chief of the Third Reich. Speer got out of his car rapidly, almost as if he didn't want to be noticed, and his exchange of salutes with the SS guards was quick and perfunctory. Like Jodl his face was pale with worry and fatigue, and unlike the professional servicemen his appearance was dishevelled and unkempt.

At the top of the stairs General Hans Krebs, Army Chief of Staff, and General Wilhelm Burgdorf, Chief of the Army Personnel Office and Military Adjutant to Hitler, stood waiting to greet the dignitaries, and it came as no surprise to them, or to anyone, that the last to arrive was Reichsmarschall Hermann Goering. Goering was wearing a curious khaki uniform, with numerous decorations and medals, and he waved his baton perfunctorily at the SS guards as they saluted, before hurrying up the stairs to greet Reichsleiter Martin Bormann, who had joined the reception party.

The crush of Nazi officials inside the long windowless corridor of the Fuehrer-Bunker began to move towards the conference rooms. Each one was stopped and his papers checked by SS guards – except for Himmler, who strode past arrogantly, alone and unchallenged, the slightly sinister steel-rimmed glasses glinting in the strong overhead lighting.

Hitler's inner clique gathered in a small, grey windowless antechamber. A large table had been pushed up against one of its unfinished cement walls and on it stood a huge birthday cake, surmounted by one tall candle. Around the cake were laid the Fuehrer's birthday offerings. There were various small, anonymous packages, but also a number of large and thoroughly conspicuous objects; the bust of a Roman Emperor, an oil painting of a naval battle, a golden tank, several large leather-bound art books and dominating everything else, a globe of painted glass lit from inside by an electric bulb and crowned by the Nazi eagle. The Fuehrer's entourage pushed for a place in front of the table, the 'inner cabinet' edging forward, the staff members and secretaries behind them.

Suddenly the murmur of conversation and the jostling ceased as an iron door swung open and a tall, massively-built man in SS uniform, Guensche, announced ceremoniously:

'Gentlemen, our Fuehrer!'

The deferential silence was broken only by the sound of boot heels scraping across the concrete floor as everyone stiffened to attention. Hitler appeared in the doorway. He was preceded by two SS men with sub-machine guns at the ready and shadowed by the young SS General Fegelein, who was his personal adjutant and brother-in-law to Eva Braun.

Hitler paused for a moment before coming into the room. Everyone, even those who knew him best, were staggered by his appearance. He was no longer the strong, self-possessed man of his public image. His face was ashen, his shoulders stooped, his jacket too big for him. Moreover since the bomb attempt on his life the previous summer, his left arm suffered from a convulsive tic which he tried to disguise by keeping his hand in his pocket. He strove to deflect attention from these defects by sheer will power and self-control. He also tried to disguise the sense of embarrassment – both social and personal – which he invariably felt on such occasions.

The room suddenly exploded with the cry, 'Heil, my Fuehrer!'

Hitler stared almost uncomprehendingly into the crowd, his eyes glazed; then the opening bars of the Horst Wessel song began, and with an effort he raised his right arm in salute and stood unblinking and unsmiling.

Goering began the ritual greetings; 'A long life and health, my Fuehrer!' he said with an ingratiating smile,

'May your undying energy and genius guide us all towards final victory . . . never, at this historical moment . . .'

But Hitler had already walked towards the next in line – Himmler. He shook his hand and looked into his eyes.

'My Fuehrer, together with the SS who in their hundreds of thousands have sworn their lives in everlasting allegiance to you, I extend my wishes – those same wishes which have always surged up from the depths of a faithful heart . . .'

Next to Himmler stood Goebbels. The round eyes protruded in the lean face; the face of a fanatic or a madman. 'I have only one wish, my Fuehrer: that destiny may grant that I remain at your side until the moment when I have to die . . .'

Albert Speer stood next to Goebbels, and a little apart: unlike the others, he remained silent, but gripped the Fuehrer's hand, and looked straight at him with a gaze that was both penetrating and unflinching. For a moment the Fuehrer's grasp was firm, and then his gaze dropped and he shuffled on down the line and halted in front of Doenitz.

'My Fuehrer! On behalf of the German Navy, always foremost in battle under your enlightened leadership, the instrument of so many triumphs of the Third Reich. . . .'

And so it continued as Hitler shambled onwards, pausing just long enough to shake hands with each man or woman; and the faces that awaited him were bright and eager, and those that watched him after he had passed were stunned by the sight of this ravaged human being – once the most energetic and most feared man in the entire world.

TWO

Immediately after his birthday ceremony, Hitler's military conference began. It was a formality. Everyone knew what the state of play was. Everyone knew the situation was hopeless. Nevertheless, the game went on.

In the Bunker conference room Hitler sat in his black, high backed chair – as always the only one seated – staring as if mesmerised at the large maps in front of him. General Jodl, the Chief of Staff, conducted the session.

'. . . in Italy, General Alexander's army has entered Bologna and is advancing across the Po valley towards Padua and Verona. In the north the English have reached the outskirts of Bremen and Hamburg. In the centre the Americans have crossed the Elbe between Magdeburg and Dessau. To the south the French have penetrated to the banks of the upper Danube . . .'

Hitler listened impassively. It was almost as if Jodl was developing one of the Fuehrer's own strategic concepts – but in reverse. Hour by hour, German-held territory was shrinking. The arrows which represented the British, American, French and Russian armies were being pushed inexorably across the map into the heart of the fatherland. Berlin itself would soon be under siege. But the worst was yet to come. The worst was always held back at these meetings since no one cared to face the Fuehrer with the ugly truth.

General Krebs took over the briefing.

'On the eastern front, my Fuehrer, in Austria, Vienna is now fully occupied by the army of Marshal Tolbukkin.

Hitler nodded perfunctorily. None of Krebs' information altered his expression. He remained inscrutable.

Goering stood beside the Fuehrer, nervous and sweating and constantly wiping his face with an embroidered handkerchief. A few feet behind him was Bormann; constantly alert and watchful. Hitler's eyes wandered over the group. The generals and the admirals stood a little to one side. He looked at them with ill-concealed suspicion. Ever since the Stauffenburg bomb plot he had distrusted them, especially now that they brought news of nothing but disaster. Their personal popularity rating had sunk lower than ever. The only group on which he felt he could rely was the SS.

Krebs paused for a moment and there was a quiet murmur among the staff officers standing at the back of the meeting.

'It seems to me,' whispered one, 'that the most important military news of the day is being overlooked.'

'Which is . . . ?'

'That Reichsmarschall Goering has apparently decided to dress from now on as an *American* general . . .'

A savage look from Bormann shut them up.

The pause became an embarrassing silence. It required courage to speak at these meetings and the Supreme Commander-in-Chief, Field Marshal Keitel, never committed himself until he had to. Now, however, he spoke quietly:

'My Fuehrer. It now remains for us to discuss the measures to be taken in the event of a meeting between Russian and American forces. This would mean the division of Germany into two.'

Goebbels seized the chance of scorching the Generals in their own fire. 'When do you conceive that such an event could take place, Herr Generalfeldmarschall?'

Keitel, as always, tried to evade a direct question of this kind. 'General Jodl, according to your calculations . . . ?'

'It isn't easy to estimate in terms of time . . . however I'd say it cannot be a question of more than days.'

The watching, waiting face of Hitler brooded over this evasive interplay of question and answer.

'How many days?' Goebbels pressed on drily.

'General Krebs, according to your latest information, how many days?'

'I am still waiting for reports from a number of divisional commands in the probable area of junction.' He indicated on the map an area round the Elbe near Torgau. Hitler interrupted. He spoke with quiet certainty, impaling them with his hypnotic stare.

'There will be no junction. I shall prevent it.'

Everyone looked at him, some with half-concealed amazement, one or two with hope. Keitel nodded and pursed his lips as if the matter were now closed, until – at least – either the next meeting or the event itself. Hitler looked calmly from one to the other of the expectant faces.

'I shall prevent it at least until I consider the moment ripe for such an event. And if and when I decide it is ripe, it will mark the decisive turning-point of the war.'

Then he raised his voice and slammed his fist on the table for emphasis, 'Communists and plutocrats will start fighting it out among themselves until it will be me who holds the balance! The destiny of Europe – of the world, therefore, will rest in my hands!'

The storm passed as swiftly as it had gathered. He sank back in his chair and Himmler took advantage of the temporary calm.

'You're right, my Fuehrer. When that happens it will be the turning-point! But meanwhile the wisest course, in my view, would be to transfer the High Command to the south with the least possible delay.'

Hitler did not react immediately. Encouraged, Jodl came to Himmler's aid.

'May I support that view, my Fuehrer? Also especially in view of the fact that we may not be able to prevent the Russians surrounding Berlin. The High Command would then be trapped – cut off from all but radio contact with the rest of the armed forces.'

'Aside from any other considerations, my Fuehrer,' added Krebs, 'this bunker is simply not big enough to accommodate the whole General Staff . . .'

Goering interrupted. 'I entirely agree, my Fuehrer. The Obersalzberg is a natural fortress, hollowed into the mountains, virtually impregnable to air attack. We must leave Berlin at once.'

Hitler sat silent, staring at something in the darkest recesses of his mind.

Ribbentrop joined in the argument. 'From a position of strength like that, when you judge the moment to be correct, diplomatic action can be initiated with either East or West as the situation requires.'

Hitler glanced at Bormann; Bormann nodded. 'My Fuehrer, forty motor cars have been ready for several hours. It needs only your order.'

Hitler's expression softened, momentarily: 'Obersalzberg . . . the place where I have spent the happiest times of my life,' he said quietly. 'Where all my great projects were conceived, where they came to fruition . . .'

Goering said, 'From Berchtesgaden, as you did before, you will organise the rebirth of the German nation.'

Hitler lowered his chin onto his clenched fists and lapsed into thought for several minutes. Then gradually his facial muscles went rigid, his expression hardened and his voice was dry, brittle and matter-of-fact.

'Leaving Berlin at a time like this would be a disastrous psychological error. As long as I remain here, Berlin will stay unconquered. Nothing can happen – nothing – while my presence is still known in the city.'

'And it will be known, my Fuehrer!' cried Goebbels. 'The whole world will know that the German Fuehrer stands fast in Berlin, at the head of the men fighting for the life of its capital!'

'We still have time,' Hitler spoke quietly. 'Plenty of time. So I shall decide at leisure . . . meanwhile in preparation for such a decision, namely to let the meeting between Russians and Americans take place, I assign the direction of government in the northern half to Grand Admiral Doenitz, with full military powers. In the south I shall entrust command of the armies to Field Marshal Kesselring, who shall none the less be subject to my direct orders. You, Himmler, with the Ministry of the Interior, will follow the Grand-Admiral to the north. Herr von Ribbentrop, you too will go to the north with the Ministry of Foreign Affairs.'

Then he turned on Goering, whose face streamed with sweat, his jaw muscles working futilely. 'Reichsmarschall Goering – you will transfer your HQ to the south.'

A sense of overwhelming relief, which he was hardly able to hide, surged through Goering.

'And never forget, any of you,' Hitler went on, 'that if the enemy advances, he must find nothing but an endless desert staring him in the face. All factories, buildings, mines, workshops, all must be destroyed!' The voice had risen to a scream.

He paused and then continued quietly, 'Herr Doktor Goebbels, as Minister for Total War, will remain with me, in charge of the defence of Berlin. Party Secretary Bormann will also stay here with me.' Goebbels' simian features twisted into a smile.

Hitler turned back to the map: 'I'll tell you one thing, Gentlemen. When Stalin decided to attack Berlin, he made the most colossal mistake of his life. Berlin will be for the Germans what Stalingrad was for the Russians. I can assure you that before Berlin the Russians will suffer the bloodiest defeat in recorded history. . . .' He flung the words at them triumphantly – a man on the verge of madness and defeat, imagining himself on the brink of greatness and victory.

16

THREE

That evening – the evening of the first day – when the others had gone, the Fuehrer gave a small 'family' party in the Bunker. Before it began, a blonde woman, around thirty, walked into the kitchen. Eva Braun was pretty and carefully made-up, like a photograph on the wall of a beauty salon. She stood in the small, cement room smoking, and talking to Fraulein Manzialy, the Fuehrer's cook. She was restless, plucking at her expensive dress, drawing quickly and nervously on her cigarette and glancing at a heavily jewelled watch on her wrist.

'It's midnight. The Fuehrer has been alive for six hours at this very minute fifty-six years ago. We must have an absolutely fabulous party tonight!'

Manzialy placidly went on with her job and took out a chocolate cake from the oven. She turned it out to cool and began to prepare a bowl filled with cream.

'God knows how he does it, that Kempke,' she remarked, 'but every day he arrives with a fresh supply of cream.'

Eva smiled and sniffed the cake approvingly. 'He's a good man all right. Now, give me something for my breath, Fraulein Manzialy. Tonight of all nights I don't want the Fuehrer to know I've been smoking.'

The cook looked at her sourly and passed her a bunch of parsley. Eva began to chew it slowly.

'God! It's bitter,' she said and then with an ingratiating smile, 'Please, how about a little something to drink, Fraulein Manzialy?'

The cook poured her a glass of schnapps in barbed

silence. Then she asked, 'Will Frau Goebbels be coming too, Fraulein Braun?'

'Of course – with her husband. Poor creature, I'm sorry for her really. Her marriage is a complete farce, in spite of all those children – all six of them. Fancy getting them all down here in the Bunker as well . . .'

She sighed with mock sadness; then she walked across to Manzialy and breathed heavily into her face. The cook drew back with as much disgust as she dared to show.

'Is that all right?' Eva asked.

'Frankly, Fraulein Braun, the Fuehrer doesn't like the smell of alcohol any more than tobacco.'

Hitler was standing in front of a mirror combing his hair when Eva knocked and went in.

'More grey hairs,' he moaned. 'More grey hairs and another birthday. Some people might think it's the Russians or the Americans who've turned me grey. It's not It's my own generals.'

Eva put an arm round his shoulders and he leaned his face against her.

'My poor one . . . poor grey wolf,' she murmured softly. 'All those worries and nobody helps you much . . . I hear they've taken Vienna. Is it true?'

'We'll be back in Vienna, don't worry.'

She kissed his cheek. 'But meanwhile . . . so much lost. And you had such a beautiful collection of antique weapons there . . .'

She went over to the gramophone, wound it up carefully and put on a record of a duet from Fledermaus. She straightened up and watched Hitler carefully.

'Vienna will be recaptured in five days,' Hitler said. His voice, momentarily at least, was resonant with conviction. Then he listened to the music, and turning to her he smiled and extended his hand. Eva, delighted, moved towards him; 'I brought that record specially from Ober-

18

salzberg,' she said running her hands through his hair, 'the only one I did bring. I'd hate you not to have your favourite record, when you have so much to worry about, poor wolf. Poor wolfie . . . I know all you're going through.'

Hitler smiled and she kissed him gently, pulling his head down onto her shoulder as carefully as if he had been a child.

Later that night the 'family' gathered in the Bunker dining room for the birthday party. It was another box of a room like all the rest; drab and grey and filled with the throbbing sound of ventilators. Conversation among the habitués lacked spontaneity but Hitler was at ease and talking fluently. The secretary who stood behind his chair recorded every word.

'When the war is over, Berlin will become the capital of the world, only to be compared with the cities of ancient Egypt, Babylon and Rome . . . this cake is truly excellent, Fraulein Manzialy,' Hitler smiled pleasantly, 'but, alas, I eat too much of it . . .'

A crumb fell onto his tunic. He looked down, frowned, and dabbed at it carelessly with his hand. A smear of cream stained the cloth.

'When I was in the front line in the last war, hunger was always with us, always round the corner. Especially for us in the infantry.' It was a favourite topic. Everyone knew what came next. 'The best invention ever made for the infantry was the field kitchen. That and that alone made my war of movement possible. That assured at least one hot meal a day for the troops.'

He was suddenly bored, and looked slowly round the circle of attentive listeners.

'Frau Christian, your dress is perfect for the German woman of today.'

Eva frowned and reached for her glass. Magda Goebbels blushed slightly and half-turned towards her husband who shifted about uncomfortably in his chair, staring down at his empty plate. General Christian flushed with pride and his wife inclined her head.

'Thank you, my Fuehrer.'

'The vanity of having beautiful or expensive clothes is not important,' Hitler went on. 'What is important is the vanity of having a well-made body, which we can all afford, all of us try and develop. When I first started my struggle, when the natural beauty of the body was distorted by monstrous fashions, you used to have the nauseating spectacle of thousands of innocent-minded girls falling for repulsive Jewish bastards with crooked legs.'

The laughter was right on cue, but scarcely vigorous. The Fuehrer's physician turned aside in an attempt to suppress a yawn.

'It is of the utmost importance to the nation that the best physical specimens should unite in giving new beauty to the country.' He looked round him, as if searching for such specimens among his audience. 'In fact the German people will reach the point of absolute racial superiority on the day when in our country alone Wagner's operas can be performed by singers, chorus and extras completely naked on stage!'

For a moment he stared straight at Magda Goebbels, until Eva Braun pushed her own chair back noisily and abruptly, cut another slice of cake, and gave it to the Fuehrer.

He tore his eyes reluctantly from Magda Goebbels, smiled absently at Braun and remarked, 'You always attend to my every need as a true woman should. A woman's world is the man. Woman seldom thinks about anything else, that is the difference. But a woman's love goes deeper than a man's.'

Then he looked directly at Eva. 'Intelligence is not very

'And the fact that he's such an inexhaustible mine of wisdom always,' Bormann was leaning over them. Then he stood up and beckoned Fegelein across. 'Come, General, your sister-in-law's pouring out some excellent champagne here . . .'

Fegelein walked slowly and thoughtfully towards them, looking at Eva thoughtfully. Suddenly he said, 'Listen to me, Eva. You're the one with the greatest influence on the Fuehrer. Probably the only one who can persuade him for his personal safety to transfer to the Obersalzberg.'

'No, Fegelein, you don't understand!'

'What *you* don't understand is that this place is about to become a death-trap for everyone inside it.'

'You over-estimate me, you see.' She looked uncertainly at each in turn. 'Or perhaps I should put it another way. If the Fuehrer trusts me, it is only because I have never sought to influence him – anyway in things which he never allows anyone to make up his mind about, except himself. I have never tried or wanted to try.'

'But surely in a case of life and death?'

'That's the most important of all, isn't it? That is exactly the question above all that he must decide for himself. And decide for me, too, come to that, because I'll be with him.'

Fegelein stared at her for a moment and then turned away.

'Come on, everybody,' Eva called out. 'It's the Fuehrer's birthday, so why don't you enjoy yourselves!'

The birthday was being celebrated throughout the bunker complex. SS guards danced with nurses and stray girls they had picked up off the streets. One woman stood out in the motley and rather drunken crowd. She was a strikingly beautiful woman in a low cut dress of great elegance. She had become known as the 'Countess', partly because no-one was quite sure where she had come from, or how she came to be there, though she was thought to be of aristocratic Hungarian origin. She was dancing with Obergruppenfuehrer Mohnke.

'I'm definitely out in the cold tonight, Herr Obergruppenfuehrer.'

'It's not apparent, Countess.'

'I was promised an invitation to the Fuehrer's party, but obviously someone saw fit to alter the arrangements. I hate bad manners.'

'Alas, Countess, the social arrangements of the Bunker are entirely outside the scope of my duties here.'

She drew closer to him.

'I've never doubted your duties were well defined, Herr Obergruppenfuehrer,' she said, putting her arms round his neck, 'and no one respects rigidity in an officer more than I do. But he must also possess the faculty of improvisation.'

'How so, Countess?'

'By turning opportunity to advantage.'

'Your breeding is as obvious as your beauty,' Mohnke said with increasing wariness, 'and yet – as officer in charge of the defence of the Reichschancellery, I must remind myself that I know very little about you. What exactly is your position in the Fuehrerbunker, Countess, if I may ask?'

'It's unique. I'm here of my own free will to be close to the Fuehrer. I'm lonely and defenceless. And in these strong arms of yours, Obergruppenfuehrer, I feel less lonely but more defenceless.'

Mohnke pressed her to him. 'I confess I enjoy the sensation, Countess.'

'Yes? Then good . . . tonight we can simply enjoy ourselves, feeling what we like, can we not, Obergruppenfuehrer?'

They scarcely moved as they danced.

Suddenly, there was a shattering explosion from a bomb falling nearby. For a moment everyone froze and stared at the ceiling. A mist of concrete dust fell slowly to the ground. The Countess and Mohnke clung to each other and still no-one moved. Then the spell broke, some-one started up the record player again and there was a ripple of slightly self-conscious laughter and talk, and the clinking of bottle necks on glass rims and the gentler explosion of champagne corks.

Hitler heard the bomb but he paid no attention to it at all. He stood dreaming dreams in front of an enormous model of a city complex. The superb, magnificent reincarnated city of Linz which would rise up in splendour at the end of the war to mark the victory and greatness of the Third Reich. And so ended the first day.

FIVE

21 April 1945. In the early morning a camouflaged army car drew up outside the Reichschancellery; its tyres ground across broken glass and rubble. A young lieutenant clambered out, carrying a big leather briefcase and wiping the dirt off his face with the back of his hand. He was unshaven, his boots muddy, his uniform creased and stained, and his face bore the signs of acute fatigue and strain. As he walked towards the entry to the Fuehrer-bunker, he tried to pull himself together, to put aside the longing to lie down somewhere – anywhere – and sleep. Wearily he exchanged salutes with the sentries, showed his pass, and was put through an exhaustive system of security checks before he arrived at the desk of General Krebs.

Krebs' aide announced him: 'Lieutenant Hoffmann from Headquarters, Army Group Vistula, Herr General.'

Krebs nodded and turned to Hoffmann who saluted. 'Any trouble finding your way into Berlin, Herr Lieutenant?'

Hoffmann hesitated, suspecting a trap, and then said, 'I made three detours to avoid Russian patrols, Herr General.'

Krebs looked at his watch. 'You have five minutes to wash and brush up, before making your report to the Fuehrer.'

'*Me*, Herr General? To the *Fuehrer*?'

'Don't worry. How you look won't matter to him. Just give a clear exposition of your maps and notes, that's all.' He turned to the aide and said, 'Show him where to wash.'

'God in heaven,' muttered Hoffmann as he followed the aide, 'I've been through plenty in the past twenty-four hours . . . but I never thought I'd end up meeting the Fuehrer!'

The aide turned and grinned at him, 'Keep calm and you'll be all right. I see him every day and I'm still alive.'

As they reached the washroom, Guensche's parade-ground yell reverberated up the corridor after them, 'Gentlemen! The Fuehrer is ready to receive you!'

In the conference room, Hitler sat back studying the huge military map in front of him. The cabinet were gathered round and everyone turned as Hoffmann entered. After a fleeting pause, Krebs carried on with the briefing until Hitler looked at him questioningly, inclining his head towards the new arrival. Krebs leaned down and whispered into the Fuehrer's ear before continuing his report. Hoffmann waited.

'As I was saying, my Fuehrer, here . . . the Russians have broken through four kilometres south of Zossen.'

Hitler seized the opportunity to play to a new and

uninitiated member of the audience. 'The advance must be stopped immediately!' he screamed.

Krebs turned uneasily to Field Marshal Keitel, who appeared not to notice.

'The fact is we have no reserves in this area, my Fuehrer,' Krebs replied and waited for the almost inevitable explosion of wrath. But Hitler had stopped listening and was studying the map once again.

Hoffmann watched fascinated. It was the first time he had seen the Fuehrer at close quarters, but he was too fresh from the realities of the front and its hopelessness to be under any illusions about Hitler, the High Command or anything else. He watched the generals and admirals waiting dutifully for the next rabbit to be produced from the conjurer's hat. Suddenly Hitler stabbed his finger at a point on the map.

'What about this unit here, Krebs?'

Field Marshal Keitel leaned over and stared down. 'Indeed, what about it, Krebs?'

'You are right, my Fuehrer – that is a reserve unit under the command of Lieutenant Kraenkel. The men are fresh and well equipped. But there are only two hundred and fifty of them.'

'What have numbers got to do with it?' Hitler cried, his voice rising in anger. 'Don't you know that two hundred and fifty Germans, led by a gallant and resolute officer, are more than a match for ten times that number of disorganized Slavs? You generals can only think in numbers. Why? Because you have no resources of inspiration or genius, so naturally you think only of numbers, figures! Do you think Caesar conquered the world by weight of numbers? When I began my National Socialist Party it counted less than two hundred and fifty members, as against sixty million citizens. When in 1934 I marched into our own German Rhineland in defiance of the Versailles Treaty, I was told it wouldn't work – our army was limited by the same treaty to a hundred thousand as against the two million strong army of France. Well, you know what happened!'

He smiled, shaking his head. He was giving one of his well tried performances. Nobody moved.

'In 1938 I was told how dangerous it would be to go into Austria – our enemies outnumbered us. I marched! Later the same year I was told that if I persisted in my policy towards the Czechs, it would mean the ruin of Germany because of the size of the armies who might oppose us. We entered Prague in peace!

'War came next year, and despite the size of their armies, we over-ran Poland and France, sent the English reeling back across the Channel, took the Balkans, entered Athens and overwhelmed Russia to the borders of the Caspian Sea! Meanwhile we had taken Norway and Denmark.'

Hoffmann watched him, now fully under the spell. Hitler's eyes were blazing feverishly, his gaze hypnotic and unswerving. Whether he was acting a momentary part, to ginger up the failing spirits of his generals, or was himself bewitched, it was impossible to tell. In any case the fascination went to work on the audience. The mood of the meeting changed entirely.

'I am fifty-six years old. Nine months ago a bomb planted by traitors exploded at my feet. Burst an ear-drum. Tore nerves out of my arm. That I lived was proof of the favour of providence. But on the world stage, providence is not enough! Mankind is ruled by the will. And when the will is thrust by genius it generates a force which throughout history has proved irresistible. Before Moscow in the winter of '41 a handful of Russians beat back our generals, numbed by fear of defeat and superstition . . . what those few Russians did to us there, we shall do here to them!'

He stood up and brought his clenched fist down on the

map. 'The hour has again struck in the destiny of the German people when the tide will turn itself in our favour. At such a turning point, can you say that a thousand men, a hundred men – yes even one man alone, is not all that is needed to enforce our historic greatness?'

They all listened hypnotised. Hitler turned directly to to look at Hoffmann to gauge the effect he had made on him. Then, after prolonging the pause for an almost unbearable time, he turned back to Krebs and said in a quiet, almost casual voice, 'Order Kraenkel to counter-attack.'

'Yes, my Fuehrer.'

Hitler leaned once again over the map. 'And now for the northern sector.'

'As the situation is so fluid there,' Krebs explained, 'I have sent for Lieutenant Hoffmann of Headquarters Army Group Vistula to give an up-to-date report, my Fuehrer.'

Krebs nodded to Hoffmann. 'Lieutenant Hoffmann, please.'

SIX

Hoffmann felt his mouth go dry. He saw a way being made for him through the press of officers and picking up his briefcase he walked forward and started to place it below the map table. But as he bent down, he saw Hitler flinch violently. Startled, Hoffmann looked nervously round the ring of faces, trying to assess what was wrong. In a spasm of intuition he realised that Hitler's mind had once again flashed back to the nightmare bomb attack of nine months ago. Flushed with misery at his stupidity, Hoffmann stood the case on the map table. With a gigantic effort of will, Hitler composed himself, stood up and stretched his hand out to Hoffmann, who shook it uncertainly and then opened the case and nervously drew out a map.

'Following the advance of the enemy armoured divisions, our forces tried to regroup here along the right flank of the Reienwalde-Eberswalde . . .'

With a sickening feeling of dismay, Hoffmann realised that he had the wrong map.

'Excuse me, my Fuehrer,' he said and searched desperately in his briefcase for the right one. Keitel and Krebs looked as if they were about to explode. Hitler remained calm, studying Hoffmann inscrutably. Hoffmann now laid a second map over the first. He started again, hesitantly to begin with, and then when he had finished outlining the position, Hitler interrupted and turning to Krebs, asked: 'What about the Oranienburg sector?'

'Everything points to Zhukov concentrating his armed forces for an all-out attack to encircle Berlin by means of a pincer movement.'

'Dr Goebbels, to what point have preparations for the defence of the capital progressed?'

Goebbels spoke with a fanatic enthusiasm. 'At this very moment, my Fuehrer, the last reserves of the Volkssturm are collecting at the assembly points. As of tomorrow, only women and girls will be permitted on the streets of the city. Every male person, regardless of age – unless holding a special pass – will be courtmartialled at once and shot.'

'Good.' Hitler turned to Krebs. 'How many tanks are available for Berlin?'

'Including those of General Weidling's Corps – forty or fifty.'

Hoffmann, still standing beside the map table, had been forgotten. He watched spellbound as the plan for the defence of Berlin developed in front of his eyes.

Again the Fuehrer dominated the discussion: 'The whole population – including the women – must start work immediately digging three lines of anti-tank ditches in all the streets of the suburbs.'

'The work has already begun, my Fuehrer,' said Goebbels. 'However, I have little faith in the commander of our forces in the capital, General Reimann. He is too cautious, too scrupulous. I don't think he's a National Socialist.'

It was the kind of thing Hitler liked to hear. He turned angrily on Field Marshal Keitel. 'Yes. He gave me the same impression. He's weak . . . or worse still he's a traitor.'

Hoffmann could scarcely believe his ears. But for once Keitel answered back. 'Oh! no, my Fuehrer! Reimann is not in any sense a traitor.'

Jodl leaped to the support of his chief. 'He's a highly experienced officer.'

'I don't want experience!' Hitler screamed. 'I want an iron will and unconditional obedience! General Reimann is relieved of his command!'

There was an astonished silence. Hoffmann couldn't think what to do – whether to stay where he was or retreat into the background. Hitler looked into the distance and asked: 'What do you say to SS Colonel Baerenfaenger?'

'He's made of the right stuff, my Fuehrer!' said Bormann, quickly and with enthusiasm.

There was a slight pause. None of the military were anxious to speak. Eventually Krebs remarked, 'Unless I'm mistaken, Colonel Baerenfaenger is only twenty-seven years old.'

'Exactly,' Hitler snapped. 'He won't have prejudices. He'll simply carry out orders. I declare Berlin a fortress. I appoint Baerenfaenger Commander of Fortress Berlin.'

An aide came in and whispered to Krebs that he was needed on the telephone. There was another awkward silence. Nobody wanted to break it, but finally Jodl said,

31

'My Fuehrer, it is my duty to point out that Berlin is not yet sufficiently equipped to withstand a siege. It may be a fortress, but it's a fortress with two million civilians inside it, all of whom must be fed.'

Hitler cut him short. 'I cannot be concerned with the welfare of civilians at this historic moment. My decisions must be determined by military considerations alone.'

Krebs returned from the phone. He was obviously nervous. 'Excuse me, my Fuehrer . . .'

Hitler gestured at him to go on.

'General Heinrici has just reported that the Ninth Army is now virtually encircled by the Russians. So he suggests moving it back before it is too late for it to take part in the defence of Berlin, where it could exert a determining effect.'

'I do not retreat!' Hitler shouted, 'The Ninth Army stays where it is. Even if it is surrounded, it must stay where it is. General Heinrici is a defeatist and a nincompoop. He understands nothing about strategy. He is relieved of his command. Is that clear?'

He turned to the map again, suddenly calm. 'I must find other troops for the counter-attack. Zhukov's forces around Oranienburg must be cut off and annihilated.'

'Yes, of course, my Fuehrer,' Keitel agreed. 'Which divisions are you thinking of using, my Fuehrer?'

Hitler pored over the map. Everyone watched him intently. Suddenly, as though he had been electrified by an idea of great brilliance, he looked up and shouted triumphantly, 'General Steiner! Steiner with his army must attack forthwith. He won't fail! Above all he's an SS man!'

'But my Fuehrer,' said Jodl, 'General Steiner's forces were intended to defend the northern sector.'

Hitler flared up again. 'I will not have my assault troops, my SS, used for defensive purposes! General Krebs, order General Steiner to instigate an attack at once. It will succeed. In twenty-four hours at the most, Steiner will have cut off the Russians from their bases. At the same time here . . .' he stabbed his forefinger at the map, 'I shall order Field Marshal Schoerner to attack from Bohemia to the north-west to cut off Koniev's advance.'

His hands thrust back and forth across the map – advancing, retreating, winning victories, cutting off enemy advances. It was another of his performances, watched with anxiety by those who would have to carry out his orders. Hoffmann watched them play their parts; he was both fascinated and appalled. Admiral Puttkammer searched the faces of his army colleagues for any signs of serious hope. But there were none.

'My intuition was right!' Hitler went on. 'I have sworn to the German people not one Russian who has dared to approach our capital will recross the Oder alive! I cannot be wrong! Everything I do and everything I say is history!'

He looked at them, watching for any sign of adverse reaction and noticed Hoffmann once again. 'What is your name, Herr Lieutenant?'

'Helmut Hoffmann, my Fuehrer.'

Hitler said to Krebs, 'General Krebs, I want your own adjutant to take the orders to General Steiner in person.'

'Yes, my Fuehrer.'

'Lieutenant Hoffmann will stay here in the bunker. He will be your adjutant from now on, and is promoted Captain.'

Hoffmann stared at Hitler, half puzzled, half proud at this unexpected turn in his life. Then he murmured his thanks, but the Fuehrer had already begun to stride from the room.

SEVEN

Later, in the mess room of the Bunker, Keitel, Jodl, Koller and Burgdorf stood talking together in an agitated group. As Krebs, followed by Hoffmann, walked into the room, Krebs said apologetically, 'I'm sorry, Hoffmann . . . I had no idea.'

' "Sorry", Herr General? But I consider it a great honour to be at the side of the Fuehrer.'

'Yes . . . of course. However, before outside communications are cut, you may wish to send a brief message to your wife and family.'

'Thank you, Herr General. I am not married.'

'Do you realise what staying here in the Bunker means . . . ?'

Hoffmann looked straight at him. There was no need for words.

Krebs said quietly, 'You can now get yourself a schnapps . . . and one for me,' and he walked across to his colleagues.

Hoffmann clicked his heels and went to the drink table. Fegelein came and stood beside him. 'Well, Hoffmann, you made a very positive impression on the Fuehrer. My congratulations. Also on your promotion. If there is anything I can do to make you feel at home here, let me know. And by the way, any time you want a drink, just take one – they're free.'

Hoffmann was puzzled. He was a Wehrmacht officer whilst Fegelein was very much of the SS, where, evidently, things were done rather differently. Fegelein underlined this by taking a cigar.

'Help yourself, Hoffmann. You can smoke in here. It's

the only place you can.' He lit his cigar and smiled. 'Provided, of course, you do it in secret.'

Across the room, the generals eased the tension engendered at the meeting by indulging in a few pointed observations of their own. Jodl in particular had had enough of fronting for Field Marshal Keitel. 'Herr General Feldmarschall, you perhaps more than any of us enjoy the close confidence of the Fuehrer: can you not tell him privately that Steiner's army does not exist?'

Keitel thought it over. 'Well, General Jodl . . . frankly no,' he replied. He took a cigar. He had no intention of being trapped in this way. 'As a nucleus, Steiner's army *does* exist. I have been thinking the Fuehrer's plan over with some care, and I tell you that if it looks somewhat chancy at first sight, his idea – as always – is the idea of a genius. And it could work.'

He lit the cigar and looked at them coolly. 'Aside from which, it's the only hope we have. The alternative is unconditional surrender to the Allies. Would you care to propose *that* to the Fuehrer?'

They all knew that this suggestion was both rhetorical and out of the question: but it served to return the ball to Jodl's court. Jodl curbed his anger and Koller asked, 'General Krebs, I should like to know the exact time of the attack and its point of origin.'

Krebs took his glass of schnapps from Hoffmann and answered, 'The time will be zero five tomorrow, and the point of origin of the main thrust will be Eberswalde.'

'But . . .' Hoffmann said and stopped abruptly. His interruption, an unforgivable breach of military etiquette, caused an icy silence. All the generals stared at him, and Krebs snapped angrily, 'You wished to speak, Captain Hoffmann?'

'Herr General!' Hoffmann was utterly confused and abashed.

'Well, Hoffmann?'

Plucking up courage, Hoffmann blurted out, 'When I left Ninth Army Headquarters, sir, Eberswalde had been in the hands of the Russians for twenty-four hours!'

The words dropped like a bomb in their midst. None of the generals looked at Krebs.

'I thank you, Captain Hoffmann,' Krebs said menacingly, and Hoffmann took the hint, clicked his heels, and walked away.

After dinner that evening, Hitler prepared to spend the night awaiting news of the counter-attack. Eva sat at the table with Goebbels, drinking a glass of beer. Fegelein and Bormann had got up from dinner, and paced the length of the dining room, talking discreetly.

Turning to Fegelein, Hitler said, 'I shall want news of the attack the minute it starts.'

Eva leaned closely towards him and said gently, 'May I stay up with you tonight?'

'If it won't make you too tired,' he touched her hair. 'I don't like you to look tired. You don't look beautiful when you are tired.'

Suddenly, they all heard a number of muffled explosions over the throb of the ventilators. It was a startling and ominous intrusion.

'What's that noise, Bormann?'

Bormann listened for a moment or so. 'I don't know, my Fuehrer. It doesn't sound like bombs.'

'What do you make of that noise, Fegelein?'

'It sounds like artillery.'

'Nonsense! How could they possibly have brought up artillery close enough to shell Berlin?' Hitler snatched up a telephone and asked for General Koller.

'It might be a long-range gun mounted on a train,' remarked Fegelein, but the suggestion did nothing to ease the sudden tension, and all eyes were on Hitler as he stared at his thoughts, waiting to be put through.

'General Koller!' he cried abruptly, 'General Koller, are you aware that the enemy are bombarding Berlin?'

'No, my Fuehrer,' Koller replied, 'I'm at Wildpark-werder.'

'People are getting worried about this bombardment,' Hitler screamed, glancing apprehensively at Eva, 'It's long range artillery. Sounds as if they have big calibre guns mounted on a train! They must have flung a bridge across the Oder to get trains across. How could you permit this to happen? Why don't you order the Stukas to attack and destroy that bridge at once?'

'There is no bridge of that kind on the Oder, my Fuehrer . . . could it be medium calibre artillery?'

Hitler's fury increased. 'Medium calibre? I won't listen to such nonsense! That would mean they're only a few miles away! Steiner must be told to attack immediately!' He looked at his watch and then yelled, 'Advance the time of the attack!'

He slammed down the receiver and looked indignantly round his court.

'How some of these generals relish bad news! They rub their hands in it! They see ghosts everywhere!'

Goebbels seized this opportunity to denigrate still more the hated generals. 'Do you know what they were passing from hand to hand when we stood in the snow before Moscow in '41? A copy of Caulincourt's account of Napoleon's retreat from Moscow! *That* was their chosen reading for the week, gentlemen!'

Bormann and Fegelein smiled sardonically at one another. Hitler shook his head sadly. ' "Medium calibre artillery!" He loved saying that . . .' He looked at the portrait of Frederick the Great hanging on the wall. 'It is never, never too late!'

'Indeed not.' Goebbels was, as always, ready with a bromide.

'You remember,' he said to Hitler, 'when I was reading

to you pages from Carlyle's *Life of Frederick the Great*?'
Hitler nodded, and Goebbels turned to Eva, in the hope
that he might impress his historical analogy upon a fresh
audience. 'It looked as if the great King was in an
absolutely hopeless situation. All his generals and
ministers believed the war was lost, and his enemies were
already carving up Prussia among themselves. The King
had given himself a few more days, then he'd take poison.
And suddenly the news came! The Empress of Russia
had died and her son had switched sides and joined the
King!'

'And on the twelfth day of April this year,' Hitler said,
'just over a week ago, that pitiful lunatic, Roosevelt, one
of the great international arch-criminals of all time, in my
opinion, died. Out of the blue – just like that! Ever since,
I've had this powerful conviction that things are going in
our favour . . .'

He stopped pacing up and down and sank on to a
divan. 'They'll regret this,' he said softly, 'that inferior
race – those Slavs. They will pay dearly for their insolence
in advancing on the Reich capital.'

Then once more his assurance returned, his voice rose
challengingly. 'I shall drive them back into the steppes of
Asia where they belong. And there they will remain for
the next thousand years!'

An hour later, the Bunker was quiet. Everyone who was
off-duty had retired and Hitler lay on his bed in the dark.
He was still in his uniform, his eyes wide open, his mind
seething with fantasies. Suddenly he reached over and
lifted the telephone by his bed. He asked the operator to
get General Koller and when Koller's sleepy voice came
on the phone, said, 'Where are the searchlights I ordered
the Lutfwaffe to transport from Prague to Berlin?'

'Unfortunately it wasn't possible to remove them because of unanticipated enemy action.'

There was a second of silence while Hitler's face screwed up in a paroxysm of violent anger. 'Very well, we shall do without the searchlights!' he shouted. 'And without the Luftwaffe as well! The entire Luftwaffe High Command will be liquidated – that will be the first order of business after Steiner's attack . . .'

It was the final order of the second day.

EIGHT

The third day – 22 April 1945, was unlike any other for two reasons. For those closest to the Fuehrer, it was the day the Hitler myth dissolved before their eyes. It was also the day on which Hitler himself came to terms with his own fate. And yet it began unremarkably.

In the officers' washroom of the Bunker, Hoffmann and a number of others stood stripped to the waist, washing and shaving. Fegelein strode in. 'Heil Hitler!' he cried, as he walked across to the nearest urinal. There was a clatter of dropped shaving brushes and razors, and muttered curses as the others responded. Fegelein said over his shoulder, 'Reichsfuehrer Himmler has sent a written message to the effect that Steiner's attack has begun.'

There was a ragged cheer. No one thought to ask why news of such importance should come through in a written message from Himmler.

'How far did they get, Herr General?' Hoffmann asked.

'Eight miles. We've got the bastards on the run, Hoffmann.'

'Terrific! Colossal!' Hoffmann's boyish enthusiasm was infectious. 'It just proves how right the Fuehrer was . . .'

The day, however, proved just how wrong all of them were.

Eva Braun was quite unconcerned with Steiner's efforts at that moment. She was having her hair done. Outside in the ruined streets of Berlin, starving women risked their miserable lives to grub about in the gutters for scraps and for firewood. But Eva's attention was devoted entirely to whether the roots at the nape of the neck – which were beginning to grow out dark – should be bleached a little more.

'The Fuehrer has always hated dowdy and ugly women.' Eva tilted her head a little to get a better view of what the hairdresser was doing. 'When he first became Chancellor, do you know what he wanted to do? He wanted all the State Ministers, Ambassadors and so on to come – not with their dull wives to the reception – but be made to come with film stars and actresses, to liven things up. But the wives made a fuss and in the end the idea had to be dropped.'

'For God's sake, Fraulein Braun,' retorted the hairdresser, 'would you mind keeping your head still.'

The Fuehrer was amusing himself by exercising his will on his shepherd dog, Blondi. The obedient animal was being ordered to march, halt and stand to attention. and carried out each command precisely. Bormann, Fraulein Manzialy and Fegelein watched the performance with admiration and it was quite obvious to them that Hitler took immense pride in the animal.

'One-two-turn! Stand to attention! March! Halt! You see . . . Blondi obeys every order I give without fail. If only my generals were as smart, we'd have won the war by now.' He sighed. 'Anyway, Frederick the Great was right. "The more I know men," he said, "the more I love dogs." You know, Bormann, Blondi eats salad too. Watch – '

He took a leaf of lettuce from a plate of green salad held by Fraulein Manzialy and gave it to Blondi, who hesitated until Hitler put a leaf into his own mouth. Then Blondi obediently ate the one Hitler had given her.

'Good Blondi,' he patted the animal, and then said harshly, 'Lie down – die!' Blondi flung herself down, her head resting on her paws.

Suddenly Hitler turned to Fegelein and said, 'Why have I had no news of Steiner's attack? Go and find out.'

Fegelein ran from the room and Hitler returned to his lyrical contemplation of his pet. 'You know, Bormann, there are times when I ask myself whether I love children as much as I love dogs. And the conclusion I always come to is, "Certainly I do." You know why? Because I cannot resist the appeal of little, imploring hands.'

He paused and paced slowly up and down the room. 'Yet I never wanted to have children. The offspring of a genius meet with enormous difficulties in life, because they are expected to show the same talents as their father. Whereas more often than not they turn out to be cretins . . . what news of your children, by the way? They're extremely bright, as I remember.'

'They are well, thank you, my Fuehrer.'

At the telephone switchboard, Hoffmann and Fegelein stood together, watching unhappily while the operator tried repeatedly to obtain the number they'd requested.

Fegelein was on edge. 'Give me the name of another centre in the same area, Captain Hoffmann.'

Hoffmann consulted his map. 'If they've advanced five miles they must at least be at Loewenberg by now.'

'I tried it ten minutes ago,' the operator said. 'There was no reply.'

'Try it again,' Fegelein replied. 'The Fuehrer insists on having news.' Then he turned to Hoffmann. 'This is your sector, your Army Group, Captain . . . the Fuehrer *insists* on having news.'

But the day wore on and still there was no trace of General

Steiner's counter-attack. Hitler sat in his study, with Bormann, Fegelein, Eva Braun, his secretaries Junge and Frau Christian and his dog Blondi. Hitler stared absentmindedly at Braun. 'You eyes are beautiful today, Fraulein Braun,' he said, but just as Eva began to respond to the gallantry, Hitler looked at the others.

'You all have beautiful eyes, ladies.'

'Oh, thank you, my Fuehrer.' Frau Christian was enraptured. Hitler helped himself to another handful of pills and Eva allowed her pique to show.

'You've taken quite enough of those pills, my Fuehrer. Dr Morell is poisoning you.'

Hitler smiled unpleasantly at the reproof. 'I shall stop the moment the war is over. Shan't need to keep up my energies then. I'll only occupy myself with Linz – the city where I discovered my artistic talent. I shall make Linz a world metropolis, with the world's greatest opera house. Also in Linz I shall build the highest bell-tower in the world. It will rise above a great crypt, which will contain my tomb.'

'But I trust you will continue to guide us with your advice, my Fuehrer?' said Bormann, unctuously.

'I don't know whether I'll have the time. Giving advice takes time and time to an artist . . .' He paused and looked at Bormann, a heavy and rather unintelligent man who depended for his advancement on craft and an instinct for deviousness. 'It's bad luck you aren't an artist, my dear Bormann, as I've so often said to you. Sometimes it worries me. You can't understand what it means to a man to have abandoned his vocation in order to restore order in his country and save his fatherland.'

He turned to Eva and put his hand over hers. 'Fraulein Braun understands that. She's an excellent photographer. She's going to help me with my work at Linz.' He smiled primly and Eva looked radiant.

Quite suddenly, Hitler snapped at Fegelein, 'What is the news of Steiner's advance?'

'Nothing new since the Reichsfuehrer's message, my Fuehrer.'

'That's not enough,' Hitler said sharply. Instinctively, everyone in the room knew that he was approaching breaking point again and that another outburst was in the offing. For a moment or so he paced up and down in silence. Then he stopped beneath the portrait of Frederick the Great and looked at it.

'Every time I look Frederick the Great in the eyes and think what he suffered, I feel like praying. But . . .' he spun round to look at his listeners, '. . . I shall learn from his mistakes. I shall not yield to the pity he showed afterwards. Until two years ago, I thought of making a clean sweep of all the Jews of Europe and lumping them on Madagascar or some other island. But today I think it is far better to exterminate them all, right on the spot, wherever you find them.'

He was interrupted by a ring on the telephone. Though Bormann and Fegelein both reached for it immediately, Hitler got there first, and pushed them aside. But he stopped and waited without lifting the phone. He stood quite still, looking at it. Then as if some important decision had been taken, he nodded at Bormann, who, surprised and apprehensive, picked it up and listened.

'Yes . . . yes, General . . .' the anxiety in his voice increased. 'Yes . . . I see.' His face froze. 'I see . . . yes, of course . . . naturally . . . Heil Hitler!'

He put down the phone. There was a terrible silence. Slowly, tightly, controlled and as threatening as a snake, Hitler looked straight at him. Bormann's eyes gave nothing away.

'So how far have they advanced, Bormann?'

'That was General Koller. No news concerning General Steiner's attack has reached him. Nor has he received any request for air cover . . .' He paused for as long as he dared, and then added quietly, 'It's his opinion that the offensive still isn't under way.'

For perhaps five seconds, no-one moved. Then Hitler exploded in fury.

'General Koller is an imbecile! Everyone knows General Koller is a perfect imbecile!'

He raised his arms to heaven in a gesture of total helplessness. 'The only general I succeed in contacting is an imbecile!'

NINE

Abusing General Koller relieved Hitler's feelings only for a short time. The appalling truth, however, could neither be disguised nor held back for very much longer. Just as it had become apparent the previous night that Berlin itself was under medium range artillery fire, so now the hard military facts – the sheer impossibility of an advance by General Steiner – could no longer be hidden tidily away.

Events came to a head at the High Command staff meeting later in the day. Hitler sat, as usual, in his black chair, gazing at the maps on which his empire was swiftly disintegrating. Keitel, Jodl, von Below, Burgdorf, Puttkammer and Krebs stood silently together, with Hoffmann and the other adjutants. Bormann, the only civilian present, kept apart, his eyes meeting Hitler's with satisfaction whenever Hitler scored a point off his hated and distrusted generals. The atmosphere at these meetings was invariably unpleasant but on this occasion it was ugly with fear and a sense of danger heightened by the fact that not one of them trusted anyone else in the room.

It was a cabal from which each of them had benefited when times were good. Now every individual present was only too uncomfortably aware of the fact that a single false step could result in the king saying, 'Off with his head!'

Krebs opened the meeting with the day's report. 'The Russians' southern wedge has penetrated south-west of Berlin, roughly towards the line Treuenbriezen Teltow . . . in the north of the city, the enemy troops are fighting in the suburbs of Lichtenberg, Niederschonhausen and Frohnau . . . still in the north the Russians have passed Oranienburg and are advancing west . . . the encirclement of Berlin should be completed within a day . . . two days at the maximum.'

Hitler looked up. The look cut Krebs short. 'I want to know the whereabouts of SS General Steiner and his army. I still haven't heard a word about the attack I ordered.'

No one replied, No one moved. Eventually Marshal Keitel, with an obvious effort, steeled himself and replied. 'Actually, my Fuehrer, the situation still isn't very clear . . . Reichsfuehrer Himmler communicated this morning that the attack was launched. But this is denied by General Koller.'

Hitler knew this and Keitel knew that Hitler knew. But Keitel was trapped in his usual evasive technique of playing for time in the hope that, meanwhile, good news would suddenly arrive. But it was too late.

'I know all about General Koller,' Hitler said calmly. 'He is a traitor.'

At the mention of this ugly word, the generals looked apprehensively at each other, trying to urge someone to speak. But Hitler stared Keitel in the eye. He had him on the hook and was not going to let him off.

'I want to know exactly where Steiner is,' Hitler said, dangerously quiet. 'Tell me how things really stand – in detail.'

Jodl came to the rescue of his chief. 'My Fuehrer . . . General Steiner managed to put three divisions together and advanced a mile and a half . . . but in order to do this, he was forced to weaken the ring of defence around Berlin . . .'

Krebs, heartened by Jodl's courage, backed him up. 'That is why the Russians have succeeded in breaking through from the north and in reaching the city outskirts.'

Hitler's face was a mask. His eyes were dark and brooding. No one could tell what was really going on in his mind.

'Steiner's three divisions are formed by detachments he scraped up from the highways,' Jodl went on, 'anyone he could lay hands on . . . men who are objectively not adapted for active service. That is why Steiner halted the attack.'

The implications behind this understatement of the appalling truth struck home with numbing force. But Hitler was unmoved. His eyes were glacial with hatred. 'This may be the truth according to the General Staff. But General Steiner is an SS officer. He would not dare disobey an order!'

Again an embarrassed silence fell over the meeting. It was time for the truth to be spelled out in one syllable. There was no escape.

'The Russians have at least fifty well equipped divisions.' Jodl struggled on with an effort which was clearly agonising to him. 'To attack them with any conceivable hope of success, Steiner would have to have a minimum of twenty or thirty divisions of men which are both fresh and well-armed.'

'It is impossible to find that number of men in all Germany,' Krebs continued. 'The soldiers are tired. The supply of provisions and arms hasn't functioned properly for months. Steiner's attack would therefore be doomed to total failure.'

46

But Hitler interrupted. 'General Steiner is an SS! The motto of the SS is "Faithful unto death" – a motto which brooks no argument!'

The generals were gagged by a sense of their own impotence. Over the last nine months their pride had been smashed and they had had to disguise and later explain to the Fuehrer disaster after disaster. Now their very lives were at stake.

'Leave the room, all of you.' Hitler spoke suddenly with an imperious gesture of his hand, 'I wish to speak to Keitel, Jodl, Krebs, Burgdorf and Bormann.'

Hoffmann, who was among the group that quickly left the meeting, was both dismayed and perplexed. The division he felt between loyalty and common sense was beginning to tear at him. Having witnessed some of the inner workings of the Nazi cabal he had begun to form a searing opinion of some of the men who were nearest to the Fuehrer. Despite his mesmeric loyalty to Hitler, the process of disillusionment had begun its inexorable work on him.

As the officers left the room, the remaining five gazed after them with envy. Once the doors were closed, Hitler placed his hands dramatically on the maps and without looking up, gave vent to his anger in a rising scream.

'An order of mine has not been executed! That is what we have come to! An order of mine has not been executed!'

He looked at the little group with flaming eyes. No one spoke. They either had to bow to the storm or perish. 'You lied to me!' Hitler continued, 'all of you, you've always lied to me . . .' He paused to allow the effect of his words to sink in. Then he raged on. 'I have been betrayed! Everyone has betrayed me! Even the SS . . .'

His hands were shaking. His face had gone purple. 'You are traitors and cowards, every one of you! There isn't a brain in any of your heads! Nothing but inflated presumption and idiocy! You – the Chiefs of the General Staff! Even you have lied to me! Betrayed me!'

The burning acid of his hatred for them ate into their fibre. The generals had long known that as a group they were disliked. But never until now had the Fuehrer been so explicit. Keitel and Jodl in particular gasped with shock; Keitel nevertheless managed to answer the charge with a certain degree of dignity.

'My Fuehrer,' he said. 'Let me honestly say that I have never at any time betrayed you. I have conscientiously executed every order you have given me.'

'And I too,' added Jodl, 'must insist that there are no grounds for such an accusation. All I did was simply put the facts before you.'

But Hitler was not listening and did not intend to hear excuses of any kind. He had begun to work himself up into a frenzy of hatred.

'You've spent years in military academies and all you've learned is how to hold a knife and fork at table! But you understand nothing – nothing about the job of a soldier! I didn't go to a military academy but I read Clausewitz and Moltke and I understood what they were talking about! I put their theories into practice. But you – who didn't understand the first word of what they were trying to say – decide to disobey an order of mine!'

Hitler leaped to his feet, turned to the wall and began hammering at it with his fists. 'I didn't even go to the cadet school but single-handed I conquered Europe and half Russia! And now you dare to disobey!'

They watched him, fascinated and appalled. He turned and faced them. 'Today of all days! Don't you know that the entire destiny of the German people for the past thousand years has been built up towards this very day, this hour, this second – and on this, of all days, you betray me! And the history of the German people for the next thousand years will likewise be determined by what happens this day, this hour and this second . . . and on this day you choose to betray me!'

He pointed an accusing finger at them all. 'Cowards! Traitors and cowards! You have been the ruin of me and the ruin of the German people!'

TEN

Outside the meeting room, the muffled sounds of what was going on inside had produced a state of shock. Scarcely anyone moved, although every person of the slightest importance seemed to have been drawn there, like iron filings towards a powerful magnet.

Hoffmann looked round. He felt distressed and helpless. All the faces round about him were frozen with shock and fear. The raging and the shouting from behind the closed iron doors continued to rise and fall. The maniac eruption they had all feared had begun and every one of them realised that the breakdown was irreversible. Everyone was at risk and each one of them felt very much alone.

Ambassador Walter Hewel, von Ribbentrop's representative from the Foreign Ministry, walked into the crowded room and went quietly up to Hoffmann. 'Excuse me, Captain,' he asked in a low voice, 'but how long has this been going on?'

Hoffmann looked at his watch. 'It must be almost three hours.'

'Was the news particularly catastrophic?'

It was a question loaded with implication, but Hoffmann did not realise this. He neither knew who Hewel was nor why he was in the bunker. Hoffmann nodded vaguely, his mind still absorbed by the event which had triggered off the fury within. 'It was the *effect*— the effect on him. That was what was catastrophic.'

'Well, what was it?' asked Hewel. Hoffmann shot him a suspicious glance and Hewel took the hint. 'My name is Hewel,' he said. 'My job is to inform the Foreign Minister, Herr von Ribbentrop.' He broke off nervously as Hitler's voice rose on a wave of fury. He turned back to Hoffmann. 'But if you'd rather I asked someone else . . .'

Hoffmann looked at him with disdain. 'The fact is that one of the Fuehrer's orders was not executed.'

Hewel stared at him. 'That's serious,' he said.

'The order was not capable of being executed in the first place,' Hoffmann replied coldly.

Hewel was shocked. 'An order of the Fuehrer – not capable of being executed!'

'Because the Generals knew perfectly well that a certain army did not exist. They lied.'

It was heresy and Hewel was shaken to the core. 'Hush, Captain . . . or you'll be in trouble . . .' He glanced round the room to see if they had been overheard. His diplomatic background had taught him that such indiscretions were not only offensive, they were dangerous.

'Someone will pay for this,' he murmured to Hoffmann. 'You'll see . . . probably someone quite innocent. Someone who had nothing to do with it.'

At that moment a burst of angry shouting from inside the meeting made Hewel take an involuntary step back. As if he himself might be in danger of becoming the 'innocent person' he had just imagined.

Meanwhile on the other side of the double iron doors, the generals and Bormann were still rooted to the places in which they were standing when the storm began. Their fear had been heightened by the physical exhaustion of standing for so long in one position. But Hitler's fury was by no means spent.

'Corruption has seeped from you down to all levels of the army,' the Fuehrer declared. 'But you'll pay for it, all of you. The same as all the other traitors have paid! You saw the film that was taken on my orders of the hanging of the traitors of the twentieth of July?' They had, indeed, all seen that gruesome film and they knew where the Fuehrer's train of thought was leading them. 'Do you remember how General von Witzleben's trousers fell off his arse when they started hauling him up to a meat hook with piano wire? Did you see the look on Helldorf's face when he came into the execution chamber and saw how it was going to be done? *Count* von Helldorf, gentlemen – an educated man, an aristocrat who went to the same schools and academies as you did, gentlemen!'

He paused to allow the effect of the picture he had painted to work. Then he thundered, 'You have brought the Third Reich to ruin! It is all your fault if I have failed!' He stared at them as if he would crush them underfoot like insects. 'I was only a simple front-line soldier in 1918 when the German politicians stabbed the German people in the back.' His voice again rose to a shriek. 'I remember how bitter you officers were! But it was *I* who resurrected the German people from the abyss. Not you . . . not the officers . . . but me and my party . . . single-handed . . . only to find now – twenty-seven years later – that it is those same officers who were so outraged in 1918 who are now stabbing the German people in the back in exactly the same way!'

He foamed at the mouth as though he were in the grip of an epileptic attack. 'But you'll pay with your blood for this! I'll have you hanged – shot – and quartered!'

The senior officers of the High Command stood like cattle awaiting slaughter. They knew that Hitler was perfectly capable of carrying out his threat. They had seen it all happen before to others and they realised only too vividly that it could happen again now – to all of them.

'I want nothing further to do with you!' Hitler shouted. 'Get out, all of you . . . I want to be left alone in Berlin! I shall put myself at the head of my troops and defend Berlin single-handed! I shall take command! *I'll* do the fighting! Get out of here.'

Hitler's final dismissive gesture sent the telephone crashing to the floor. He stood still for a moment, staring at it. The blood which had suffused his face a deep red now began to drain away, giving place to an unnatural pallor. He sank slowly back into his chair and stared vacantly at the map of Germany spread out in front of him. His eyes began to swim with tears. They travelled slowly and forlornly over the ravaged scene and the tears began to trickle down his cheeks as he stared at one of the little flags on the map on which the word 'Steiner' had been printed.

As if speaking to himself alone, he murmured softly: 'It's all over . . . the war is lost . . . my Third Reich has collapsed . . . I must kill myself.'

Then, suddenly, he broke down completely, crying bitterly. He could no longer control himself. His face sank forward on to his arms. His shoulders heaved. The raging tyrant was suddenly a shrunken and pathetic man in the depths of unreachable despair. Even his body seemed to have shrunk, so that his uniform had become too big for him and emphasised his helplessness.

The impact of this incredible sight brought about a change in those left watching. Their terror gave way to shock. Not one of them could believe what he saw. The whole ethos of the myth collapsed and vanished like an evil stench. They were shattered. The very source of their life had run dry and none of them knew what would happen next.

Quietly and discreetly one figure detached itself from the group and walked away. Bormann let himself out through the door.

ELEVEN

To those outside, the sudden silence, which had followed the Fuehrer's collapse, seemed more terrible than his furious screaming. The door opened and Bormann slipped out, closing it quietly behind him. Goebbels grabbed him and said in a low voice, 'What's happened? What was it about?'

But Bormann was too shocked to answer. He stared uncomprehendingly at Goebbels and the rest of them, without really seeing anyone. Then, as if in a dream, he said 'A mint tea. Quickly! The Fuehrer needs some mint tea.'

Within moments Frau Christian hurried from the kitchen with a tray of tea and some cups. She made her way through the outside room and, followed by Goebbels, entered the meeting room and went across to the desk.

She poured out a cup and was about to put it down beside the Fuehrer when she noticed that the map in front of him had been smudged by his tears. She started from surprise but she managed to keep the emotion which welled up in her under control. 'Some mint tea, my Fuehrer . . . it's nice and fresh . . . and piping hot.' Her voice shook slightly.

Hitler did not react. He sat there like a waxwork, his white tear-stained face staring hopelessly into space. Frau Christian passed on the cup of tea to Field Marshal Keitel. 'Herr Feldmarschall Keitel . . . ?'

She poured another cup, 'Herr General Krebs . . . ?' Krebs shook his head politely and firmly.

'Don't you like mint tea, Herr General Krebs?'

'Yes . . . I . . . very much . . . only I never really drink at this hour.'

The incredible round of politenesses continued. Frau Christian placed another cup beside the Fuehrer who heaved a long, soulful sigh. Mechanically he lifted the cup and bent his head towards it. He took a sip, but it was too hot and he dropped the cup carelessly back on its saucer. Frau Christian looked alarmed. She poured a cup of tea for herself. No one spoke.

Finally Frau Christian could stand it no longer. 'It's still a bit hot . . .' she coaxed, 'but this way it does the most good.' She might have been coping with a difficult child.

After a few seconds the Fuehrer began slowly to sip the infusion.

'Is there enough sugar, my Fuehrer?'

Hitler looked up and answered with a polite nod.

'Yes. You make a very good cup of tea, Frau Christian. Excellent,' beamed Keitel, idiotically.

Jodl looked at his chief with such withering contempt that Keitel winced and turned away. As soon as Hitler had put his cup down again, Jodl spoke in a voice which betrayed the depths of his feelings.

'My Fuehrer, for six years of war we've served under you. For this last decisive battle, therefore, we await your orders. You can't just send us away.'

Hitler remained locked away in an inanimate, obstinate silence. He appeared not to have heard. Frau Christian began to gather up the cups and left the room. Jodl pressed on. 'Without you we are lost.'

There was still no reaction from Hitler.

'Besides – the position is not quite as desperate as it looks. Two whole Armies are still intact. In Southern Germany . . .'

Krebs, the only other general with something approaching courage, interrupted Jodl. 'General Jodl is right, my

54

Fuehrer. Schoerner's armies in Czechoslovakia are completely intact.'

'Then there's Kesselring's army in Italy,' Jodl added.

Keitel plunged in. 'The overall situation isn't at all as dramatic as it appears from here in Berlin. Earlier we presented only the negative aspects . . .'

'It is all over . . . I will remain in Berlin . . . I will die here.' The voice was a flat monotone.

But having at last got him to speak, Jodl determined to win him round. He continued patiently, 'My Fuehrer, if we shift the forces fighting in the west towards the east and abandon western Germany to the English and Americans, we can save Berlin from the Russians and drive them back across the Oder . . .'

He paused. There was no reaction. He went on cautiously, as if picking his way across a minefield. The others watched admiringly, but without envy. 'But this, of course, means transferring the supreme command to the centre of the armies, to a position which is impregnable – the Obersalzberg . . .'

Hitler shook his head. 'I will not leave Berlin . . . I will die here . . . if you want to go, then go . . . I will die in Berlin . . .'

'But, my Fuehrer, allow me to repeat . . . we have the men and we have the arms to carry on the war. You have only to give the orders . . .'

'I have no more orders to give . . . if you need orders, ask Reichsmarschall Goering. '

Jodl answered with indignant contempt. 'There is not one German soldier who would fight and die for Goering!'

A glint of satisfaction lit Hitler's face momentarily before he retreated once more into his cocoon of unshakeable obstinacy. 'What exactly do you mean by fighting?'

He paused, hoping that Jodl or one of the others would take the bait. But they all kept quiet.

'At this stage there is no longer any question of fighting . . . there is nobody willing to do it.'

Still none of them argued back.

'If it comes to negotiations, Goering can do it better than I . . . so go, all of you . . . I don't want to look at you . . . get out of here! . . . I want to be alone with Goebbels.'

TWELVE

So the die was cast. The generals of the Third Reich saluted and left their Fuehrer alone with his 'familiar'; the small, dark-eyed madman, Goebbels.

Outside the meeting room, an attempt was being made to get the ordinary routine of the High Command going again. Hoffmann approached Krebs, notebook in hand, ready to take down orders in the usual way. But before anything could happen, Eva Braun ran into the room, white faced and breathless. She flung herself at General Fegelein, her brother-in-law, who recoiled with embarrassment.

'Where is the Fuehrer? What is the Fuehrer doing?'

Fegelein pointed at the inner sanctum and bending down, murmured something about a 'crisis'. Eva looked round wildly and Frau Christian went over and put a consoling arm around her shoulders.

'Fraulein Braun . . . oh God, it was so terrible! The Fuehrer was in tears . . .'

'My God, no! That's never happened before. Why? What did you all do to him?'

It was not a question that anyone cared to answer and Frau Christian led her gently away.

As their footsteps died away, Hoffmann turned once

more to Krebs. 'The orders, Herr General?'

'None.' Then, thinking he had, perhaps exceeded his brief, he looked at General Jodl. 'Wait . . . General Jodl, what orders to give?'

But Jodl had had enough. He snapped back, 'It is Feldmarschall Keitel's duty to issue the orders.'

'Orders?' Keitel said, as if this were the last thing in the world he expected to be asked, 'But . . . the Fuehrer never said anything at all.'

'Exactly,' said Jodl. 'In that case it's up to you.'

Keitel was trapped. What was worse, his brother officers and Bormann knew it and were relishing it. 'Really . . .' Keitel stammered, 'the situation is very complex . . . Herr Bormann! You, who have always been so close to the Fuehrer . . .'

'Close?' Bormann said craftily, 'well, yes, of course I've been close . . . but I'm not in a position to make *military* decisions. After all, you're the Chief of the Supreme Command of the Armed Forces.'

They all looked at Keitel and waited. The Field Marshal cleared his throat and looked around despairingly. He could detect no help coming from any direction.

'But, gentlemen!' he burst out, 'the situation is impossible! It would be madness for any of us to make decisions. All we can do is wait until the Fuehrer gets over his crisis . . .'

'There is no time to wait,' Jodl said curtly. 'Somebody must tell the Fuehrer at once that by his behaviour as a member of the armed forces he could be charged with desertion!'

It was an astonishing remark. No one had thought of it before. There was a sense of almost comic relief until Jodl whirled round on Bormann and barked, 'Bormann, *you* are his right hand . . .' The implication was plain.

The heat was on and Bormann began to stammer. 'Really . . . quite honestly . . . I . . . I wouldn't even know how to begin raising an issue like that, the way he is.' It was an act of abdication. The way was open to lesser bidders in the power auction.

Krebs said, 'The Fuehrer told us to ask Reichsmarschall Goering for orders . . .' It was a signal for the jockeying for position to begin.

'In a moment like this,' Fegelein interrupted, 'there is only one man who can do anything at all . . . Reichsfuehrer Himmler! I shall go and ring him at once.'

He ran from the room and General Christian followed him, remarking as he left, 'I must ring Reichsmarschall Goering and inform him immediately as to what the Fuehrer said.'

Admiral Voss got up from his chair. 'In my opinion, our only hope is the immediate and responsible intervention of Grand Admiral Doenitz.' He followed the other two.

General Burgdorf waited until Voss had left, then he remarked, 'We'll have to help the Fuehrer to get back his self-confidence. The best thing would be to contact his old Party friends and comrades – Ley, Rosenberg, Todt . . .'

'Herr Todt has been dead for years, General Burgdorf . . .' Bormann snapped irritably.

'I'm sorry,' Burgdorf stammered, embarrassed. 'That of course, I know. I meant to say Herr Speer.'

'He won't encourage the Fuehrer,' Bormann growled, 'Speer would be worse than useless!'

'The obvious person is Herr von Ribbentrop.' Hewel hurried out, followed by Burgdorf. Only Keitel, Jodl Krebs and Martin Bormann remained. And not one of them needed to be told that very little time, and even less hope, remained.

THIRTEEN

Hitler did not change his mind. He was determined to stay in Berlin, and later in the day, Dr Goebbels drafted and recorded the Fuehrer's message to the people of Berlin.

'The Fuehrer personally assumes the defence of Berlin. He will fight to the very last breath! The Fuehrer will win or die, but he will remain at the head of his troops!'

Outside the world of the Fuehrerbunker the steady reduction of Berlin to a vast heap of rubble continued. Starving women and children picked over the trash in the gutters, vying with the rats for scraps of food and leaving the dead to rot where the bombs had struck them down. The holocaust was appalling and showed no sign of relenting, but this was another 'truth' to which Hitler did not expose himself. Things were very different beneath thirty feet of protective concrete.

There was a tiny closet-like room in the Bunker. in which there was just enough room for a telephone switchboard and a small camp bed. On the bed the Countess and a very handsome young SS officer lay tired and dishevelled, locked in each other's arms.

'I wish we could stay here forever,' he whispered, kissing her passionately, 'Never – never leave . . .'

'Oh! yes,' she murmured, 'you make a woman feel totally isolated in a world of your own. I'd rather be here in your arms than anywhere I've ever been or could be . . .'

Her passionate declaration was proved false rather sooner than she expected. For a moment or two she gave herself utterly to the pleasure of reducing the young officer to a state of almost anguished ecstasy; then there was a discreet knock on the door. The expression on her lover's face turned from ecstasy to panic.

'Don't answer,' she whispered, and he shook his head in a vehement denial of any such intention. The door handle was tried, but the door was locked.

Then there was a discreet cough and a voice from outside said, 'Is the Countess there, by any chance?'

She kept her finger on her lips. There was a tense pause. Then the voice outside said, 'Because the Fuehrer would like to see her in his private apartment.'

The effect was electric. The Countess flung herself off the bed and started feverishly to arrange her dress. She was so determined not to miss the occasion for which she had waited all her life that she unlocked the door and her bed-mate got awkwardly to his feet as an even younger SS officer entered.

'Heil Hitler!' said the newcomer, without a flicker of surprise.

'Heil Hitler!'

The Countess flung her arms round the younger man and gave him a hug. 'Putzi! You arranged this for me?'

He nodded proudly.

'I won't forget this,' the Countess said, 'you'll see . . . I keep my promises, too. You'll see tonight.'

'But now hurry up, if you please, Countess.'

'You mean I won't have time to change?'

He shook his head. Cursing, she struggled to pin up her hair. It made very little difference. She was still a ravishingly attractive woman, whatever the state of her hair or her clothes.

'Well, really!' she said as she almost ran out of the room, 'I know Bunker society isn't all that *comme il faut*, but all the same you'd have thought a lady would have been given the chance to make a proper toilette . . .'

In the small meeting room of the Bunker, Hitler greeted the ladies of his dwindling court. He bowed as he kissed the hands of Magda Goebbels, Frau Christian, Fraulein Junge, Fraulein Manzialy and two or three others. Just before the outer door closed, the Countess rushed in breathlessly, and tried to compose herself. Hitler kissed her extended hand.

'Thank you, my Fuehrer.' She smiled radiantly. 'I've been living for this moment since childhood. Since then I've thought of nothing else.'

The Fuehrer's smile was formal, ice-cold. Then he turned to address the group. His face was grim with suffering. 'My dear ladies,' he began, 'I have asked you all to come here in order to say goodbye. In an hour's time a plane will be ready to fly you south. So please lose no time in making your preparations.'

There were startled cries of protest. Hitler made an imperious gesture with his hand.

'*Yes.* Because this place will soon be an inferno – certainly no place for ladies.'

The women looked at one another aghast. Then Frau Christian declared firmly, 'My Fuehrer . . . I shall stay with you . . .'

'I have no intention of leaving, my Fuehrer,' Fraulein Junge said, and Fraulein Manzialy with an affectionate, motherly and slightly exasperated smile cried, 'However could I leave you? Who would make you take your drugs at the right time?'

'Staying behind in Berlin,' he pronounced, 'means that I shall fight at the head of my last faithful soldiers – then die.'

'If that's how it must be,' Fraulein Junge said, 'I shall die with you.'

'So shall I, my Fuehrer,' Frau Christian added.

'No matter how hard the circumstances, a woman's duty remains unaltered, my Fuehrer.' The Countess's eyes were bright with unshed tears – but the remark caused one or two raised eyebrows among the rest of the group.

Magda Goebbels ignored this attempt at pathos and said sincerely, 'You know very well, my Fuehrer, that I shall never leave you.'

'That I know is true.' He was very moved and in order to keep control of himself he forced himself to be curt. 'But if it is an order?'

'For the first time I should refuse to obey one of your orders, my Fuehrer.'

'So should I . . .' It was a unanimous pledge of devotion.

The Countess added disarmingly, 'I am at your *entire* disposal . . . if there is anything I can do for you . . .'

The emphasis on the word 'entire' was faint, but unmistakable. Hitler could no longer hide his emotion. He looked first at one and then another and then said in a weak and tremulous voice, 'Thank you, ladies. I cannot force you against your will . . .' He paused and then sighed, 'If only my generals were as brave as you.'

He dismissed them and walked into his private study, where Eva Braun and Guensche were waiting. Hitler stopped and stared at them. Quite suddenly he had forgotten why he had asked them to be there. Eventually Guensche said timidly, 'The papers, my Fuehrer? You were going to select what is to be kept and what destroyed.'

'Ah, yes, Guensche, the papers . . .'

Slowly and as if every breath he took cost him an effort, Hitler began to sort through the papers in his private files. Guensche had provided two wooden boxes and took the documents as Hitler handed them to him; laying the ones to be kept carefully into one box, and ripping up the rest and throwing them into the second. Eva Braun curled up in an armchair and began to sift through a sheaf of photographs. Though everyone else was showing signs of acute strain and fatigue, she continued to look uncannily untouched by the whole ghastly experience. She remained pretty, beautifully dressed and totally relaxed, a porcelain dummy capable of nothing but the most superficial sentiment. After a time she stood up and handed Hitler a few photos.

'What about these, my Fuehrer?'

Hitler looked at them. His eyes misted over and he looked down for a moment, trying to compose himself. After a moment he said, 'These we shall save, Fraulein Braun . . . I don't want to happen to me what happened to Christ . . . future generations must know exactly what I looked like, and it must be the truth. I don't want over-exhuberant artists to depict me with blond or red hair, or any nonsense like that.'

He handed over the photographs to Guensche, and resumed his examination of the files. Suddenly he stopped, picked up a thick sheaf of typewritten pages and began to read them with increasing concentration. His eyes shone, his hands began to shake with excitement and he could scarcely keep hold of the pages. 'Listen to this, Fraulein Braun . . . and you, too, Guensche! It's Dr Wulf's horoscope . . . he was a scholar, a friend of Himmler . . . it dates from 1930.'

He began to read. 'The war will begin in 1939 and will mark great victories for Germany until 1943 . . . then come years of defeat . . . the hardest blows will be struck in the first months of 1945.' He looked up for a second. They were both listening attentively.

'In the second half of April there will be a series of fateful events . . . great events for Germany, which will precede a period of calm until the first days of August when peace will be concluded . . . during the three years which follow, Germany will live through a hard period, but from 1948 on, it will arise again in triumph . . .'

By now Hitler's eyes were blazing feverishly. Braun and

Guensche looked at him in amazement. 'When mystery coincides with reality,' he said portentously, 'it is a sign that providence is intervening. It is the sign that the mystery itself has become revealed truth . . . it is the revelation of our ultimate victory!'

There was little sign of Germany's ultimate victory as the third day drew to an end. Hitler called an additional session in the meeting room and produced another plan, inspired by his reading of Dr Wulf's horoscope. Keitel and Jodl took the brunt of his ranting once more.

'Wenck . . . Wenck's army here on the Elbe . . . south-west of Berlin.'

'Yes, my Fuehrer.'

'It must be disengaged from the Americans . . . at once . . . this very day!'

'Yes, my Fuehrer.'

'It must fight its way back in the direction of the city . . . and arrive here at the Chancellery.' His eyes became feverish as the plan developed in his mind.

'The Twelfth Army is my own personal creation . . . I have faith in General Wenck.' He paused and then asked, 'What is the situation of the Ninth Army?'

'Still fighting around Frankfurt on the Oder,' Jodl answered.

'The Ninth Army must immediately be prepared to attack west, to join forces with Wenck's Army . . .'

Keitel, anxious to please as always, remarked, 'A perfect plan, my Fuehrer . . . if you will allow me, I shall go to General Wenck personally to co-ordinate the meeting between the Ninth and Twelfth Armies.'

Hitler ignored this, so that Keitel did not know at first whether the Fuehrer agreed to his going or not.

'You, General Jodl,' Hitler glanced again at the map, 'will take charge of the attack in the area north of Oranienburg.'

'Yes, my Fuehrer.'

Hitler and Eva Braun

Top   Alec Guinness plays the title role in the film, *Hitler: The Last Ten Days*

Right   Hitler, the orator, in a characteristic pose

Top   Magda and Joseph Goebbels with their six children

Bottom   On 28 April 1945, news of Himmler's offer of surrender reached Hitler

'I shall leave immediately, my Fuehrer,' Keitel said, but there was still a questioning note in his voice.

'No.' Hitler paused to enjoy the effect of this on Keitel. Then, quite suddenly, in an entirely different tone he said, 'First you must have something to eat. To give you strength for the journey.'

He rang the bell and Guensche came in. 'Guensche, have them prepare a good solid meal for Feldmarschall Keitel. At once! I shan't tolerate delays!'

He looked down at the map again. The great area of victorious Germany had been reduced to a small circle, marked by a coloured pencil. Keitel and Jodl watched him. But as always, the Fuehrer's inmost thoughts remained a mystery even to those who worked most closely with him.

Half an hour later, Hitler presided in the dining room as Keitel struggled through the food that had been prepared for him.

'A little more mayonnaise, Herr Feldmarschall?' Hitler enquired, as if they were at some late night supper party in peace time. Keitel accepted graciously and then started as Hitler suddenly snarled, 'See to it that my orders are carried out without weakness or mercy! The only effective remedy for retreats is executions. Don't confine yourself to shooting ordinary soldiers. You will need to go higher up – generals, if necessary!'

'Yes, my Fuehrer.'

Then, equally abruptly, Hitler admonished Keitel gently. 'Don't eat so quickly, Feldmarschall! It isn't good for the digestion.'

Overwhelmed by this touching concern, Keitel became embarrassed, and to cover his confusion, blurted out impetuously, 'My Fuehrer . . . I . . . I can't hope to express my admiration . . . only a man of exceptional character like you could have recovered his will at a moment when all seemed lost.'

Hitler accepted the compliment in an urbane but friendly manner. 'More salad, Feldmarschall? My intuition tells me that at last we are on the road to success.'

'I couldn't be more sure about that, my Fuehrer . . . I'm absolutely certain . . .'

The noise of renewed bombardment thundered through the Bunker but neither Hitler nor Keitel paid any attention. Fraulein Manzialy came into the room and placed a small package on the table.

'I personally gave instructions to have something prepared for you for the trip,' Hitler explained. 'What is it, Fraulein Manzialy?'

'Sandwiches and a little wine.'

'Please put in a bar of chocolate, Fraulein Manzialy. I want Feldmarschall Keitel to reach Wenck in top form.'

He pointed at a small bottle. 'Take that cognac along too . . .'

Keitel was delighted.

Hitler smiled. 'Ah! – but it's a quarter of a bottle only . . . A private can get roaring drunk but a field marshal mustn't have more than a drop to warm him up . . .!'

Suddenly, Hitler scraped back his chair and offered Keitel his hand. 'Good luck, Feldmarschall Keitel . . .'

Keitel got to his feet and clasped it warmly. 'We shall meet again at the liberation of Berlin . . . Sieg Heil, my Fuehrer!'

So Keitel and Jodl left. The staff car, a large Mercedes, drove slowly through the city, its lights out. The driver bent forward to watch out for craters and rubble and avoided the worst of the obstructions by the light of the burning city. The Field Marshal and his Chief of Staff sat close together – their faces grim.

'There is only one thing I can tell Wenck,' Keitel

remarked, glancing at Jodl. 'The final battle for Berlin has begun. Everything must go into it. The Fuehrer's life is at stake.'

Jodl took no notice of the trite remark. He was deep in thought and for a moment or so did not even answer. When eventually he did, he made no attempt to disguise his disillusionment. 'There is something I will confess to you, Feldmarschall,' he said, looking straight ahead into the darkness, which was lit only by the intermittent flashes of gun fire. 'I was very much disappointed by the Fuehrer's incorrect behaviour today. I had always considered him a soldier and at the very moment when he should have assumed the final responsibility he let himself go like that . . . this hysterical rage, those suicide threats . . . all that sloppy carry-on. He behaved more like a prima donna than a Commander-in-Chief.'

Keitel looked at him but said nothing.

'A soldier receives orders,' Jodl went on, 'and a soldier gives orders. That is what a soldier is! I'm not sure I shall ever get over a disappointment like that . . .'

Keitel's only reaction was to light a cigar and continue staring straight ahead of him. There seemed to be nothing else to say.

FIFTEEN

Late that night, in Eva Braun's room, Magda Goebbels sat wearily in an armchair, listening to the voices of her six children playing in the next room. Eva sat filing her nails. 'It will be a great comfort to me, Frau Goebbels, and I mean it sincerely – having you come and live here with the children . . .' Eva sounded as if she were planning years of companionship.

'Thank you very much, Fraulein Braun.'

Magda tried to disguise her despondency. Eva noticed and was irritated by it, but went on filing her nails and then, glancing at herself in the mirror, she let out a wail of dismay. The zip in her dress had begun to come undone.

'Oh! damn the thing,' she said. 'This dress is practically new . . .'

She groped ineffectively with it, trying to pull it up. Magda beckoned her across, 'Come – I'll help you.' Her voice sounded tired.

Eva strolled over and Magda fiddled with the zip. 'Try not to be too worried, Frau Goebbels . . .' said Eva, softly. And then, 'Dear Magda . . . may I call you Magda?'

'Why, of course, Fraulein Eva . . . Eva, I mean . . . I'm not worried for myself. I can face the end. And it goes without saying my husband can . . . it's the children.'

Eva was twisting and wriggling to try and help Magda get the dress done up. She hadn't listened to what Magda said and missed the point completely. 'Well, of course it'll take them a few days to adjust. Anyway it'll all be over soon. You'll see – we'll be laughing about it one of these days.' She reached for the zip, 'Here, let me have another go.'

She moved aside, tugging and pulling, but obstinately the zip remained jammed. She went on in disgust. 'These dresses are a complete and utter disaster. Suits or uniforms are better for down here. It's just that they don't suit me. You have some lovely ones, though, Magda.'

Magda was watching her children through the open door, and hadn't taken in any of Eva's prattle.

'I just can't get it to budge. I'll have to change.' She slumped down in her chair and said, 'Thank goodness the Fuehrer has got over that appalling meeting. He's been through a ghastly time, poor lamb. He even asked me to go back to Munich, but of course I wouldn't let him finish the sentence.'

Magda pulled herself together, and smiled bleakly. Eva sat up and had another pull at her dress. She looked bad-tempered and childishly sulky.

'Wait till I have one more try,' said Magda soothingly. 'Hold it very straight and tight . . . there . . .'

'I must say I'm much happier in my mind. A while ago General Burgdorf told me we have at least fifty chances in a hundred of victory. He also said he doesn't often lose a bet. What's important is – the Fuehrer's got his confidence back. That's all that matters.'

Eva picked up her nail file again, 'Oh! yes, it's only when he "believes" in himself that we can go on holding our heads high and not get desperate . . . Oh! How divine! You've got it!' She dropped the file and clapped her hands with delight and stared happily at her reflection in the mirror. 'Thank you, Magda . . . you're an absolute marvel!'

Hitler sat alone in his study, hunched in his chair, staring at the maps. Himmler's personal doctor, Gebhardt, who was waiting, somewhat impatiently, for an audience with the Fuehrer, sat outside talking to Bormann.

'I hope you succeed in persuading the Fuehrer to leave at once, Herr Doktor.'

'I hope so. I hope so.' Doctor Gebhardt was clearly preoccupied with something quite different. 'Will he confirm my appointment, Herr Bormann?'

'Probably. Though why you should want such a job at this particular moment, I can't imagine.'

Dr. Gebhardt smiled deprecatingly, 'It's just that . . . I've coveted it for a long time.'

'Yes,' said Bormann, 'and I can see why, Herr Doktor Gebhardt.'

'You can see *why*, Herr Bormann?'

'It will give you something of the status of a neutral –

like a kind of honorary Swiss citizen – immune from the consequences of anything you may have done before.'

Gebhardt's face flushed. But Bormann was not a man to take chances with, and he bit back his anger. 'That is *farthest* from my thoughts, Herr Bormann, I assure you.'

An aide came from Hitler's study and asked Gebhardt to come in. He got up and went through the doorway apprehensively. He was amazed at his own nervousness. His usual sang-froid deserted him. He was transfixed by the penetrating stare and hardly knew how to begin.

'Reichsfuehrer Himmler is on his way to see you, my Fuehrer. Meanwhile he has sent me to point out the advantages of your immediate transfer to Obersalzberg . . . he says that in Bavaria . . .'

Hitler interrupted curtly. 'My decision is irrevocable. I shall remain in Berlin.'

'In that case, Reichsfuehrer Himmler suggests transferring at least Fraulein Braun to Obersalzberg . . . and the other ladies . . . my aeroplane . . .'

'The ladies living in the Bunker have decided to stay with me until the arrival of Wenck's army.'

Dr Gebhardt looked down at his feet and coughed nervously. He was not getting on very well. Hitler's interruption had abruptly dried up the flow of speech which he had hoped would carry him to his objective.

'Anything else?' the Fuehrer asked.

Dr Gebhardt nervously put a hand in his pocket and took out a sheet of paper. His hand shook slightly as he did so, a fact which did not pass unnoticed by Hitler. 'Actually, my Fuehrer, there's this new appointment of mine . . . subject to your confirmation, of course . . . my appointment as President of the German Red Cross.'

Once again he was paralysed into silence by the coldly amused stare of Hitler's ironic and searing eyes. He cleared his throat and stumbled on. 'Reichsfuehrer Himmler told me of your decision to appoint me . . . you see . . . I mean . . . as Head of our Red Cross.'

Hitler said nothing but continued simply to look at him. Gebhardt felt impelled to justify this request. 'As the Reichsfuehrer's personal doctor, I have always carried out the most delicate orders to the letter . . . I have prepared hundreds of "special treatments" on dangerous prisoners . . . I am one of the most ardent supporters of experimenting on human guinea pigs. Results with animals are not really reliable.'

He began to regain his confidence and allowed himself a little justifiable pride. 'The concentration camps offer such vast human material that it is a pity not to use it for the perfecting of German medicine. Your own doctor, Dr Stumpfegger, my Fuehrer, will confirm it. My gas gangrene experiments on prisoners were a *success*. And so were the bone grafting experiments on Polish girls, the tests with poisoned bullets, the sterilisation of people belonging to inferior races . . . a list of my other successful experiments would run into hundreds, not to mention all the orders which I faithfully executed.'

Once again he ran out of words as Hitler's obstinate, ironic silence unnerved him. Then he took a deep, rasping breath and struggled on, 'So that is why Reichsfuehrer Himmler thought I would be the right man for the appointment of President of the German Red Cross. But if you think . . . so then . . . you won't confirm it?'

But Hitler had amused himself with this exercise of power long enough. He had other things to do. 'Of course it's confirmed, Dr Gebhardt. You are the new President of the German Red Cross.' He signed the piece of paper. 'Only don't come to me asking for better conditions for prisoners of war. When it is necessary to abandon a POW Camp, I don't want my soldiers to drag dead weights along after them.'

'I understand what you are saying, my Fuehrer.' Gebhardt was smiling obsequiously. 'Prisoners will be disposed of where necessary without being moved.'

A little later SS Commandant Berger was granted a brief audience. Hitler had not moved from his chair, and was no more pliable with Berger than he had been with Gebhardt.

'Reichsfuehrer Himmler will be coming here personally as soon as possible,' Berger began. 'In the meantime he has sent me to explain his point of view. Reichsfuehrer Himmler is deeply concerned about your personal safety. He does not consider it advisable for you to remain in Berlin . . .'

Hitler interrupted with a gesture of irritation. 'No. I've announced that I'm staying here. And that's all! Anything else, Herr Berger?'

Berger, crestfallen, tried again.

'Reichsfuehrer Himmler has further ordered me to be in Bavaria tomorrow to handle the question of the prominent prisoners . . . the war prisoners of a certain eminence . . . and the question of a few separatist ring leaders . . . Movements like the one which has broken out in Austria.'

Hitler was stunned. 'Separatists in my adopted country – and in my native land!' He paused and there was an edge to his voice. 'You must be very severe with them.' He yawned. 'And who are these prominent prisoners?'

'The former President of the French Republic, Lebrun, Daladier, Herriot, Léon Blum, Gamelin, François-Poncet, King Leopold of the Belgians, the son of Stalin, Churchill's cousin, de Gaulle's sister . . . Princess Mafalda of Savoy died on the 19th April . . .'

'She was the rottenest of all the Italian royal family.'

Berger nodded. 'I wish to know, my Fuehrer, whether you agree to my departure for Bavaria. Or would you prefer me to stay here in Berlin? It would be an honour to fight at your side.'

'No. Go to Bavaria. Go . . . Goodbye, Berger.'

Berger saluted. 'Heil, my Fuehrer . . .' He turned and was walking towards the door when Hitler suddenly stood up, his left arm shaking as it hung lifeless at his side. His head was shaking too, and in an unexpected explosion of wrath, he shouted, 'Shoot them! Shoot them all!'

Berger hesitated only for a moment, and then ran out, closing the door behind him. Outside, Bormann was waiting for him. He put a hand on the SS officer's shoulder and said, 'Well? What is the Fuehrer going to do? What did he say? Will he leave Berlin?'

'Absolutely not. Not a hope.'

Berger lowered his voice and then went on: 'But he gave me an order I don't quite know how to interpret. About the groups of prisoners – the so-called "prominents" and the Austrian separatists. He said, "Shoot them all". But all of whom? The prominents or the separatists?'

Bormann was exasperated at the stupidity of the question. He shrugged his shoulders and said cynically, 'In case of doubt – shoot them both. That way you can't go wrong.'

SIXTEEN

By the fourth day – 23 April 1945 – the Fuehrerbunker was almost literally under siege. Of the senior members of the Nazi hierarchy, only Bormann and Goebbels remained. Communication with the outside world was reduced to one underground cable.

The booming of artillery was closer and very nearly continuous. The Bunker itself had not yet come under direct fire and during the day it was still possible to go out into the grounds. Eva Braun, Magda Goebbels and Frau Christian sat in the garden in the weak April sunlight and watched the Goebbels children playing with Hitler's dog among the bomb craters.

But it was almost the only light-hearted moment in an otherwise darkening time. Down below in the meeting room, Hitler presided over a dramatically reduced 'court'. SS General Fegelein, Goebbels and Bormann remained, but of the Wehrmacht contingent, only Generals Krebs, von Below, Admiral Voss and the disillusioned Captain Hoffmann were left. Just as previously they had waited for news of Steiner's attack, so now the Fuehrer and his entourage awaited news of General Wenck's liberation of Berlin.

Meanwhile, Fegelein read out to the Fuehrer the latest batch of messages. '. . . Reichsfuehrer Himmler has been delayed en route for unavoidable military reasons and hopes to reach the Bunker as soon as possible. He urges you to consider transferring to Obersalzberg in order to continue the final struggle.'

Hitler listened with ironic indifference. He waved his hand in the supremely bored way of someone who had heard it all before. 'Next?'

'Doctor Ley begs you to continue to keep the destiny of Nazi Germany in your hands – '

Hitler raised his eyebrows at Fegelein, who continued quickly, ' – by establishing your headquarters in Berchtesgaden.'

Hitler dismissed this with yet another disparaging gesture.

'Doctor Rosenberg reaffirms his confidence in the final victory and the triumph of the pure race – and urges you to consider leaving Berlin at least for the time being . . .'

'Never,' Hitler snapped. 'Continue . . .'

'Admiral Doenitz praises the efficiency of the troops he

has in charge. They are ready for the decisive battle. He awaits your orders, my Fuehrer. He will call you tomorrow at Obersalzberg.'

'Where he won't find me. Continue.'

'Field Marshal Kesselring hopes to meet you as soon as possible in Munich, where he will join you during the day from Italy.'

Hitler shrugged his shoulders. 'Is that all?'

Fegelein nodded dejectedly. 'For the moment, my Fuehrer.'

Hitler looked at them all in a glazed way. He was not amused. 'Well, gentlemen, sometimes I take time to reach a decision but once my mind is made up, nothing changes it. I can confirm the fact that I shall stay in Berlin. We stand at the threshold of victory. Wenck's army will liberate the capital.'

His listeners remained silent. Nothing had changed in the previous twenty-four hours and still there was no good news to alleviate the strain. All that had happened was that the circle around Berlin on the map was smaller than ever.

The door opened abruptly, and Bormann entered, followed by Goebbels. Both of them were in a state of great excitement. 'Forgive me, my Fuehrer,' Bormann said, 'but a radiogram has just reached us from Reichsmarschall Goering.'

Hitler greeted this piece of news with an expression of bored irony. 'I thought someone was missing . . . very well, let's hear it.'

Bormann read the telegram as if he was addressing a public meeting. 'My Fuehrer, in view of your decision to remain at your post in the fortress of Berlin, do you agree that I take over total leadership of the Reich, with full freedom of action at home and abroad, as your deputy, in accordance with your decree of the 29th of June 1941? If I should receive no reply by 10 pm this evening I shall infer that you have been deprived of your freedom of action and shall consider the conditions of your decree as fulfilled. May God protect you and speed you here safely in spite of all. Signed your loyal Hermann Goering.'

By the time Bormann had finished reading, his voice had pitched itself high with suppressed anger. Hitler, however, showed no particular reaction. He simply sat and listened and stared with unfocussed eyes at the maps in front of him. Then he waved at Krebs and the other officers to go out. Hoffmann was the last to go. He closed the door carefully behind him with a long, curious look at the Fuehrer.

Hitler was left alone with Bormann and Goebbels, and Bormann raged on immediately. 'Goering is a traitor, my Fuehrer! His action amounts to a coup d'état. Not only that but he has sent similar telegrams to all the members of the cabinet to inform them that unless he hears otherwise, he will take your place tonight at midnight.'

'Tonight at midnight,' Hitler murmured to himself.

Bormann produced another telegram from his pocket. 'Here is one received by Herr von Ribbentrop – who is now waiting outside.'

'I don't want to see Ribbentrop. Absolutely not! Give me the telegram.' He was terribly agitated.

Bormann hastily handed the cable to him. Hitler took it, read it over in silence and then looked up. 'I've known it for a long time. I knew that Goering was rotten. He corrupted the entire Luftwaffe. He allowed corruption to seep through the entire State. He's been taking morphine for years! I've known it a long time . . . a long time!'

'He must be shot. At once, my Fuehrer.' Bormann looked just a little too eager.

Hitler stared at him for a moment or so, saying nothing; then, to the surprise of both Bormann and Goebbels, he shook his head energetically. 'No, not that. No, no, no . . . we must not supply the world with more pro-

76

paganda material against Germany. There is enough of that already.'

He paused and looked at his two closest associates, both of them hanging on his decision with vulturine eagerness. 'But I remove him from all his offices. He is deprived of the right to succession. Draft him a telegram to that effect, Bormann.'

Grinning with satisfaction, Bormann sat down at the table, heedless of formalities, and feverishly began to write Goering's dismissal on the back of his own telegram.

SEVENTEEN

It was the fifth day; 24 April 1945. In the radio room of the Bunker, the operator was broadcasting an announcement '. . . Following a serious heart attack, Reichsmarschall Hermann Goering was obliged to resign into the hands of the Fuehrer all his military and political offices . . .'

In the meeting room, Krebs was giving the first of that day's reports. 'Since the first light of day, the Russians have attacked on all sides. At ten hundred hours they succeeding in cutting the road between Berlin and Nauen, our only remaining outlet to the east . . . Berlin is now completely surrounded.'

He waited for a comment from Hitler, who watched him with a blank, expressionless face.

A junior officer slipped into the room and signalled to Hoffmann to follow him out. Hitler stared after his retreating figure. Krebs decided to go on. 'We can still communicate with the outside world by means of an underground telephone cable. It is, however, the only one which is still intact.'

Hitler's glazed stare now fastened on Krebs. 'Where is Wenck?'

'Wenck's Twelfth Army still hasn't succeeded in forming a continuous front. Nor in gathering the requisite strength for the attack on Berlin.'

Hoffmann came back and Hitler shifted his attention to him. It took a certain amount of prodding from Krebs before Hoffmann could bring himself to speak. 'My Fuehrer, I have been informed that Tempelhof Airport, as a result of intensive fire from enemy artillery, has been put out of action.'

Tempelhof was the last effective airport. So there was no longer a safe way out of Berlin, even if the Fuehrer had decided to change his mind and evacuate himself and his staff to the south.

'However, since the first hours of this morning, my Fuehrer,' said Goebbels encouragingly, 'an OT battalion of one thousand men has been working to transform the East-West Avenue at either side of the Victory Column into a landing strip . . .'

'By his failure to defend the airport, it is obvious that Colonel Baerenfaenger is incapable. He must be relieved of his command.' The voice was harsh. Hitler turned to Burgdorf. 'By whom, General Burgdorf?'

Burgdorf was embarrassed. 'It isn't easy, my Fuehrer. Three Commanding Officers have already failed in one week. In my opinion the best remaining choice is General Weidling.'

'Very good. I nominate General Weidling Commander of Fortress Berlin. Have him report to me.'

Burgdorf saluted and left. Hitler turned to Krebs. 'General Krebs, I am disappointed with the Ninth Army. Their advance is too slow. Inform General Busse that my orders are to advance rapidly at all costs – regardless of losses.'

Krebs was stunned. The rest of them stared down at

the floor, utterly dismayed and perplexed. Hoffmann began to think that what he was experiencing surpassed his wildest nightmares.

Hitler thundered on. 'The time has come when the life of no German soldier must be spared! It is the duty of every soldier to shed his blood! The Russians must find themselves attacked from all sides and thrown into total confusion, so that they won't have time – so that they will have neither the time nor the means – to organise any effective resistance. Then Wenck will be able to enter Berlin in four days!'

There was no comment which any of them could make on this insane speech.

Hitler now turned to von Below. 'Von Below, I want Luftwaffe General Ritter von Greim to take a plane immediately and present himself to report here at this bunker tomorrow morning!'

'Yes, my Fuehrer!'

With Tempelhof airport out of action, von Below permitted himself a look of surprise at this order. Even the use of the East-West avenue as an airstrip was, at best, bound to be problematical.

'Any questions?' Hitler snapped.

Fegelein leaped to attention. He was hesitant and embarrassed. 'Yes, my Fuehrer . . . on behalf of Reichsfuehrer Himmler and Grand Admiral Doenitz, I wish to report the proposal of Gauleiter Wegener.' Getting no encouragement, he nevertheless carried on. 'He asks if you, my Fuehrer, would approve of a partial surrender to the west, to the English and Americans, to reinforce the anti-Russian front and therefore avoid a two-fold devastation of Germany.'

Hitler reacted with fury. 'I surrender to nobody! I do not understand the meaning of the word "capitulation"! I shall never hand over to a pack of degenerate Jews everything that I have achieved in ten years of ferocious struggle!

'In fact, it is not my desire at all to avoid devastation. Eleven years ago I said to the German people, "If we cannot conquer, then we should drag half the world into destruction with us! There will not be another 1918" . . . So – if Germany must die, it will go down in a heap of ruins! If they have been too weak to face the test of history, they are fit only for destruction, and will go down in a sea of flames to illuminate the Viking funeral of the Reich!'

He paused, suddenly calm. Hoffmann stared at him in total incredulity.

'In any case,' Hitler went on, 'Wenck's troops will get here first. I am sure of that, Fegelein.'

The day wore on and in the late afternoon Eva Braun, Frau Christian and Fraulein Junge walked up into the garden for target practice. Fegelein and Hoffmann went with them and loaded their pistols. They fired at a life-sized scarecrow, dressed in the uniform of a Russian soldier, which jerked and flopped as the bullets hit it. Their screams of delight were nearly drowned by the thunder of the bombardment.

Frau Christian shot first. 'Die, you stupid Slav!' she yelled.

Then it was Fraulein Junge's turn. 'I'm not afraid,' she declared. 'I'll never allow any Russian soldier to come anywhere near me.'

Eva Braun eyed the target coolly. 'The best thing is to aim at the neck. It's the safest and it isn't hard to hit. We'll stop them at the doors of the Bunker!'

EIGHTEEN

It was early on the morning of the sixth day – 25 April 1945. An official from the Ministry of Propaganda had been brought into the first briefing. He was trembling with excitement. 'I heard it myself, my Fuehrer,' he began, with my own ears. It came over a Swiss radio station.'

He paused, both for effect and because he was out of breath. Then he stumbled on. 'At the moment of junction between Russian and American troops in the heights of central Germany, violent arguments arose between the commanders of the two armies over the occupation of the captured territories.'

Everyone in the room was riveted. Hoffmann stopped taking notes. Fegelein, Burgdorf, Krebs, Voss and von Below couldn't take their eyes off the little man, who went on, 'The Russians have charged the Americans with breaking the agreements. It appears there has been some shooting.'

Hitler's eyes began to flash and sparkle again. A look of satisfaction spread over his face and he even managed a smile. 'That's quite natural,' he said. 'I knew it would happen. Only an idiot like Churchill would believe in an alliance with the bolsheviks. Not even you understood when I refused to allow our armies to retreat and ordered them to hold out. Well – now you have the reason.'

He stood up. 'Wouldn't the German people, wouldn't history itself brand me as a criminal if I concluded a peace at the very moment that the struggle between ultra-Marxists and ultra-Capitalists has begun?'

He was shaken by emotion. He clenched his fists and

banged them down on the maps spread over the table. 'We still have considerable forces in Norway, in Italy and in Czechoslovakia . . . we can recall them, and establish them around the capital to wait for the inevitable conflict between the Russians and the English and Americans . . . and I shall be the referee, the sole adjudicator of the world in balance.'

Then, with a gesture of dismissal, he began to pace up and down the room. Perhaps after all, the horoscope was coming true and fate was making a direct intervention on his side.

All day he could think of nothing else and that night he developed his theory to its ultimate conclusion. The court sat at table in Hitler's study, with cups of tea, the inevitable chocolate cake and an open bottle of champagne. Eva, the Goebbels, Bormann, Fegelein and two secretaries were listening quietly to the customary monologue.

'I know there are people who are so fired by their enthusiasm for the resurrection of the German people that they look on me as a prophet, a second Mohammed, a second Messiah. I must reply, with the utmost sincerity to all these good people, that I am absolutely *not* a prophet nor am I a Messiah.'

He took another bite out of his cake. 'I am a genius – yes. A Messiah – no.'

He smiled briefly at Eva Braun. 'Do you see me, Fraulein Braun, in the role of Christ?'

Eva shook her head, and smiled.

'Concerning this business of people's fanaticism towards me, I must confess that it isn't merely a question of being regarded as a Messiah, which would only be a minor evil. The truth is – popularity is a perpetual torment . . . there is nothing I curse more . . .

'That is why I have had until now to give up all ideas

of getting married . . . from 1931 until today I have been the slave of my duties, of my concern for the wellbeing of the German people, whom destiny has entrusted to me . . . had I been married, there would be moments when I would be forced to say: "What do I care about my wife?" and I should have always had before me a face filled with suffering and pain . . . that is why it is better for me never to marry.'

He put his hand in his pocket, took out a little silver box and extracted two pills. Eva looked worried and confused, began to speak, stopped, and then tried again. 'My Fuehrer . . .'

But Hitler took no notice of her. He swallowed the two pills and plunged more fervently into his peroration. 'It is always better to have a mistress. Naturally that is valid only for exceptional men like myself . . . I don't believe that a man like me could possibly marry. A man of my stature has created an image of the ideal woman in his mind, taking the body of one, the hair of another, the intelligence of a third, the eyes of a fourth . . .'

As he spoke, Hitler's eyes wandered first to one woman and then the next. Eva looked down. Her hands were clenched in her lap.

'But it is always an ideal creature which does not exist.' He spoke as if with genuine regret. 'One must be satisfied with what beauty one single woman has to offer.'

Eva Braun's eyes filled with tears of hurt and confusion.

Suddenly there was a tremendous explosion. It seemed to shatter the Bunker. Instinctively everyone looked up at the ceiling. There was a moment of undisguised terror. A heavier blast followed the first. The ceiling remained undamaged but the room filled with swirling dust and fumes.

Fegelein rushed to the door shouting to Guensche to have the ventilators turned off. The fans were sucking in the clouds of dust and sulphur. Everywhere – in the corridors, kitchens, washrooms, the anteroom with the adjutants, the smoking room and the SS Mess Room, people were coughing, their lungs choked with dust and fumes.

Hoffmann pushed past the groups of frightened retching people and made his way up into the garden. He stood in the darkness staring at the crater left by the two huge explosions. An SS officer came up and stood beside him and together they gave the gaping cavity a long and very worried look. Both of them smoked and for a while said nothing. Then the newcomer said: 'Captain, you take part in the Fuehrer's staff meetings. You should persuade him to leave the Bunker – just once. Even half an hour would be enough. He'd see the dead with his own eyes. He'd know what Berlin has been reduced to, and what people are saying. When he went into that Bunker, he left a different world behind him from the one he'd find if he ever came up again!'

He paused and then added, 'If the Fuehrer asked me, I'd give him an honest answer.'

But Hoffmann only shook his head and went back inside, followed by the SS officer. To their surprise, as they reached the bottom of the steps leading into the corridor they found several officers milling about excitedly, drinking and laughing. The bald-headed old man in livery, who had functioned as a receptionist, was joining in with gusto. They all began to shout, an exuberant chorus, 'Sieg Heil! Sieg Heil! Sieg Heil!'

Hoffmann buttonholed a soldier. 'What happened?'

'A plane! A plane has actually landed in Berlin! At the Victory Column . . .'

'Unbelievable! Drink to it, Captain!' cried an officer, waving a bottle at him.

Hoffmann snatched up a glass. 'What type of aircraft?' he asked.

'A Fiesler-Storch with General von Greim and Hanna Reitsch! She piloted him in!'

'Christ almighty!' Hoffmann said admiringly. He drank deeply and let himself be carried away by the atmosphere of insane joy.

NINETEEN

But General von Greim did not reach the Bunker until the following day. On 26 April 1945, a group of soldiers, prudently wearing Red Cross armbands, carried in a stretcher almost at a run. On it lay von Greim, his foot shattered and swathed in blood-soaked bandages.

He was a thin man with a pale, gaunt, proud face. He was dressed in his Luftwaffe General's uniform and wrapped haphazardly in a blood-stained blanket. Beside the stretcher walked a woman in pilot's uniform. Hanna Reitsch was small, attractive and very feminine, in spite of her determined features and fanatical eyes.

The General was carried into the bunker surgery where Hitler's personal doctor was waiting. Dr Stumpfegger examined the wound and then set to work. The general was in great pain but Hanna Reitsch stayed with him, talking softly to him, running her hand through his hair with the tenderness of long, deep intimacy.

'I'll be lame for the rest of my life. Never be able to fly,' he groaned.

'What do you suppose I'm around for? Why did you pick the best pilot in Germany after yourself?' She smiled at him. 'You'll get them to build you a special plane,' she went on, 'and we're going to pilot it together.'

There was a clatter of footsteps in the corridor. Reitsch and von Greim both looked round. The Fuehrer came into the room and the general made a heroic and rather comic effort at a military salute.

'Heil, my Fuehrer!'

Hitler smiled fleetingly and walked over to the operating table. 'How is our patient, Dr Stumpfegger? How long will he take to get over it? Will he be able to walk again?'

But before Dr Stumpfegger could answer, Hitler turned to von Greim and bending over him said earnestly, 'Thank you for coming, General. It was your right to disobey that order. It may even have struck you as unreasonable from where you were.'

The general made a valiant effort to smile in spite of the pain. Hitler, however, was studying Hanna Reitsch. 'That was courageous of you, Hanna Reitsch! And typical, too! You have saved the life of one of my best soldiers. Thank you.'

He gave her an approving nod and turned back to the General. 'It was an excellent idea to bring her along.'

'Bring her?' the general said. 'She won't leave me! She hasn't for years . . .'

Hitler looked curiously at Hanna. 'I know, I know, General von Greim . . .'

It sounded like some sort of ambiguous reproof. Neither of them understood it. Hitler went on, 'There was a time when Fraulein Reitsch used to visit me very often . . . we'd enjoy a chat about old times . . . a very charming companion and a true and gallant friend.'

The magic of Hitler's personality worked again. Hanna's face was transformed. Hitler's words seemed to spark off a latent flame of passion in her.

'I really came to Berlin to see you, my Fuehrer,' she said in a low, emotional voice. But he turned away. Hitler had forgotten her. He bent over von Greim. 'Do you know why I asked you to come here?'

'No, my Fuehrer.'

Hitler began to tremble with rage. 'Because Hermann Goering has betrayed me and his fatherland. He has sent me an insulting telegram . . . an ultimatum! An ultimatum to me! . . . His behaviour proves the depths of his villainy.'

He was screaming and his eyes were swimming with tears of self-pity. Hanna watched him with sympathy; von Greim with immense indignation. 'Whoever would have expected treachery like that? And from Goering!'

'He sent me a telegram.' Hitler held the offending piece of paper in his trembling hand. 'He reminds me that at one time I had named him my successor. At this of all moments he had the effrontery to think he could take my place! Read it for yourself . . .'

Von Greim took the telegram and tried to read it. Hitler's face twitched with rage.

When von Greim finished the telegram, he looked at Hitler in perplexity. The effect of it on him was obviously quite different from the effect on Hitler. He simply could not understand the implication.

'An ultimatum . . .' Hitler raged on, 'a vulgar ultimatum! Now there is nothing left. Nothing is spared me! No faith, no honour! There is no bitterness, no betrayal that has not been heaped upon me . . .'

Von Greim temporised. He still didn't understand why he had been summoned to the Bunker. But Hitler fell silent as swiftly as he had been provoked and von Greim tried testing the ground.

'My life is at your entire disposal, my Fuehrer! Unfortunately now it is the life of a cripple, but I shall do everything in my power to carry out any order you give me . . . tell me, my Fuehrer, tell me what you want me to do.'

'General Ritter von Greim . . . I appoint you Commander-in-Chief of the Luftwaffe with the rank of Feldmarschall. In the name of the German people, I give you my hand.'

Von Greim was totally confused and overwhelmed. He struggled to speak. 'My Fuehrer . . . my gratitude for such a high honour overwhelms me . . . but I don't know if I shall be capable of assuming so great a responsibility.'

'If you were not worthy of my confidence, I would certainly not have chosen you.'

There was a long, embarrassed pause. Hitler did nothing to relieve it. Eventually, von Greim felt compelled to ask, 'And now, my Fuehrer, tell me . . . I mean . . . why did you summon me here from Munich?'

Hitler looked thoroughly irritated; as though the reason must be obvious. 'Why? To tell you of your appointment!'

'I am deeply honoured, my Fuehrer . . . but surely – I mean – you might have sent me a telegram . . .'

Hanna Reitsch's feminine instinct made her break in quickly, 'The Fuehrer needed to look you in the eyes, General . . . to "feel" your loyalty by personal contact, to console him in this moment of great bitterness . . .'

Hitler was delighted with her. 'I shall put all the available fighter planes at the disposal of my new Commander-in-Chief of the Luftwaffe. It is immaterial how many planes it is necessary to sacrifice to escort you to your new place of command! The Luftwaffe is expecting you. Everyone awaits your orders to bring the accounts of war to a definite and victorious close!'

'Yes, my Fuehrer.'

Hitler was suddenly struck by a last-minute thought. 'I want everything to be in order before you leave. I shall send you my personal tailor to make your Feldmarschall's uniform.'

His eyes rested on Hanna; and then on von Greim. 'Why don't the two of you get married?'

'My Fuehrer, the General and I are happy the way we

are.' Hanna Reitsch smiled radiantly and for a brief moment seemed soft and gentle, 'and besides I don't believe in marriage – when one has other interests in life which take first place – I'm not bourgois enough for marriage.'

'I understand perfectly, Fraulein Reitsch . . .'

Her face lit up with pleasure.

Hitler turned to go. 'I'd be very happy if you'd both join me at my tea party this afternoon . . .' He walked away down the corridor.

Stumpfegger, with a sigh of relief, finished stitching the wound and began to dress it. Von Greim seemed no longer to feel any pain. He lay back staring at the ceiling, an expression of amazement on his face.

'Goddamit, I still can't understand why he made me come here . . .'

He took Hanna's hand. 'It's all very well, but we've lost a hell of a lot of planes – and we've both risked our lives . . .'

TWENTY

The tea party took place in the late afternoon in the Bunker dining room. Dr Goebbels, Martin Bormann, Eva Braun, Magda Goebbels and the secretaries were all there. The sense of unreality was total. Everyone behaved as if they were gathered in any German or Austrian middle-class home in peacetime. Yet the cups and plates and cake stands laid out on the table rattled constantly because of the continuous shelling and bombing outside.

Von Greim was brought in by two Red Cross orderlies. Hanna Reitsch followed him and Hitler turned to her and kissed her hand with exquisite courtesy.

'Welcome . . . welcome . . .' he said. Hanna, whose hair was beautifully dressed and who was fully aware of her glamour and personality, looked round happily, with a touch of triumph in her smile. Then Hitler said, 'May I introduce Fraulein Braun?'

Hanna shook hands casually, scarcely looking at her, and then smiled a 'hello' to Magda Goebbels and the others, who moved aside to make way for her. To her amazement, Eva Braun invited her to sit next to Hitler.

'Something to drink, Fraulein Reitsch?' Eva asked her politely.

'Yes, I'd love some tea.' She found it hard to hide her fascination – and irritation – at seeing these two together.

But Hitler was interested in only one thing. 'Now, Fraulein Hanna, we're all waiting for you to tell us about your flight to Berlin. Aren't we, Fraulein Braun?'

'Oh, yes!' Eva said with a nervous smile. 'I'm sure it will be fascinating!'

'Perhaps that's not the ideal word to describe it,' Hanna snapped. 'It was sheer hell.'

It wasn't quite the reaction they had expected from the celebrated aviatrix. Nevertheless, Hanna continued in a dry and hostile voice, without once taking her eyes off Eva. 'We started from Reichlin packed into a single seater Focke-Wulf 190 and flew to Berlin. General von Greim refused to leave me behind.'

'He has a noble heart,' Eva interrupted ironically.

Magda Goebbels chided her. 'A loving heart, Fraulein Braun . . . right, Hanna?'

'Yes,' Hanna agreed. She had been caught momentarily off balance. 'For years . . .'

She stopped abruptly and there was a slightly awkward pause. Then she tossed her head and went on. 'He put me into the tail of the fuselage through a safety hatch. There were fifty fighter planes in the sky to keep the Russians off. I myself saw over forty shot down.'

She looked down for a moment as if she didn't know how to go on. 'When we arrived at Gatow in Berlin, we got into a red Fiesler-Storch trainer and roof-hopped towards the Chancellery. But at the Brandenburg Gate we took a direct hit from an AA shell. It shattered the General's right foot, while he was piloting.'

Eva Braun winced slightly and Hitler took hold of her hand, trying to reassure her affectionately as if she were a nervous child.

'Fraulein Reitsch is an amazing woman,' he said.

Hanna stopped what she was saying, disconcerted by this sign of intimacy. Then she said, 'It was touch and go . . . I crawled forward and grabbed the controls and we managed to put down on the main East-West axis.'

For a moment Eva was genuinely moved. 'Incredible! . . . but how absolutely marvellous! You are an amazing woman, Fraulein Reitsch, the Fuehrer is right.'

Hanna did not answer.

'Will you be staying here with us now?' Eva asked her.

But Hitler answered, 'No. The Commander-in-Chief of the Lutfwaffe must take personal charge of organizing air cover for the Wenck offensive.'

He stopped abruptly, filled by sudden misgiving. 'Where's Fegelein, Fraulein Braun? Have you seen him today?'

'No, my Fuehrer,' Eva said innocently, 'When he said goodnight last night, he told me he was going back to his command.'

'I must call him,' Hitler said, 'and if he rings you, tell him I want to see him. He must arrange for the departure of the Feldmarschall and the faithful Hanna.'

He smiled at Hanna. With an effort, she smiled back. Meanwhile, without a trace of irony, Eva said blandly, 'It's really a shame you're not staying, Fraulein Reitsch. I've only known you a few minutes but I'm sure we would have become great friends.'

TWENTY-ONE

Later that night, Hanna Reitsch went to say goodnight to the Goebbels children. All six wore immaculate brown Nazi uniforms. She kissed each one of them and they bowed and kissed her hand.

'Sleep well.'

The smallest, a little girl, said 'It doesn't mean we're going to *sleep* yet.'

'And why not?'

The little girl hesitated, 'Well, first there's the bombardment.'

'Don't worry – you're safe down here, little one.'

'The "bombardment" is what they call their pillow fights,' Magda Goebbels explained. 'Half an hour of pillow fights before they go to sleep. It does them good to let themselves go a bit . . . they were so used to running about all day.'

When the children had gone, leaving Hanna and Magda alone, there was a long silence. Magda knew what was going through Hanna's mind but did not open things up. At last Hanna said hesitantly, 'Is . . . uh . . . is she . . . I mean Fraulein Braun . . . you know . . . and the Fuehrer?'

Magda nodded.

'But she's so bourgeois,' Hanna said indignantly, 'not a bit like a National Socialist. She might be some receptionist in an Austrian beauty-parlour – until you hear her talk, that is, and then you think she can't have left school.'

Magda spoke in a low voice as if afraid of being overheard. 'They've been together ten years.'

Now Hanna was shattered. 'But you can't mean they're really . . .' she broke off.

'Really lovers? Yes, I suppose they are.' There was a twinge of malice in Magda's voice.

Hanna gave a shudder of revulsion. A shell burst up above but neither of them paid any attention.

'How extraordinary! . . . and I'd always thought his spiritual nature above things like sex.'

'I wouldn't know if he is *in* love with her . . . I used to explain it away to myself by saying "perhaps he just relaxes with her" . . . I suppose you could say she's the sort of mediocre creature it's easy to be with when you're tired . . . but now I'm not so sure.'

Hanna got to her feet and stood with her back to Magda looking at a picture on the wall. Another shell burst overhead. Magda couldn't resist a final dig.

'You look awfully put out, my dear . . . I'm so sorry if I've said anything to upset you.'

Hanna smiled wanly. Then, without another word, she left and went away to her quarters.

Hitler sat at his desk, absorbed in the pile of charts which was spread out in front of him.

Eva Braun came in carrying a tray. She spoke quietly to him. 'Aren't you going to bed, dear?'

'No . . . I still have things to do . . .'

'Please, darling,' her voice was filled with concern, 'do at least stop work for a moment and have a little tea. If you only knew how I worry about you, seeing you so tired out and hardly sleeping at all . . . you're always working.'

As she put down the tray she realised that Hitler was not studying military maps but architectural plans which he was touching up with a special pencil.

'Adolf! You're really the most incredible person!' she

cried, in surprise and admiration. 'Even with the situation as it is, you can still think of the future, your art . . . my dearest, darling little wolf . . .'

She ran her fingers through his hair, kissing his cheek over and over again. Hitler didn't respond. He was still concentrating, still absorbed.

'Wars – and men – come and go, Eva. What remains are only the great buildings. The Colosseum, the Parthenon and the Pyramids . . .' He showed her one of the drawings. 'I have a small structural problem,' Hitler explained. 'The colonnade inside the Linz Opera House . . . see? I don't want it to interrupt the grandiose scale of the entrance hall . . . if only Speer were here . . . he understands these things . . . we could have discussed it.'

'What a pity for the world,' Eva said with the sublimity of the truly ignorant, 'that you couldn't have devoted your life to art . . .'

TWENTY-TWO

It was 27 April 1945. Outside in the rubble that was once Berlin, two SS guards tried to put up a notice on what was left of a wall.

'Soldiers of Wenck's Army – the People of Berlin know that you have reached Potsdam. Hurry and help us!' On the ground beneath it, one of their colleagues lay dead, his face spattered with blood. The two guards ran back to cover, leaving the body where it was.

In the Bunker staff mess, Hoffmann sat at a table, propped on his elbows, an uncapped bottle by his side. He still took notes for General Krebs, still passed on orders, but he watched what was happening around him with undisguised distrust. He was well on the way to being drunk, like the majority of people in the mess room. A couple of young SS officers sat opposite him.

'What's the use of all of us sitting around on our arses waiting for Wenck's army to turn up?' he asked them belligerently. 'I mean to say, it's cowardice . . . if there's ever going to be a moment for us fellows in the Bunker – a moment to do anything decisive, it's *now*. We should go up and attack the Russians at the same time as our own troops are hammering at them from Potsdam. This idea of sitting around under thirty feet of concrete, drinking and eating, when there's fighting to be done . . .'

He broke off. The two SS officers had sprung to attention. He felt a paternal hand laid upon his shoulder, and turned to find Bormann smiling at him. Hoffmann pushed himself up on his feet and came to attention. 'Heil Hitler!' he said.

'Heil Hitler . . . well, that's the stuff, Captain. I like people who show a fighting spirit. And I won't forget it. People like you, faithful to the Fuehrer, who stand by him in this Bunker in his darkest hour – such people will be offered the highest offices of State, yes and titles of nobility, too . . . all these people here . . .'

Bormann's arm waved extravagantly round the room. Hoffmann listened to him with growing amazement.

'As soon as our struggle is brought to a victorious conclusion,' Bormann concluded, 'you may depend upon it, Hoffmann.'

Bormann turned complacently away and a cynical smile crossed Hoffmann's face. He took another drink, and a long hard look at everyone standing being 'faithful to the Fuehrer'. He felt sick with disillusionment.

Things were different with von Greim. The new field marshal sat near the telephone switchboard, his leg propped up on a chair, and spoke to General Koller at the front.

'No, my dear Koller . . . I won't have you talking like that . . . you must not despair . . . everything will come out all right . .'

He broke off. There was an impassioned outburst at the other end of the line. Von Greim waited till Koller had finished, then he said soothingly, 'I used to think that too . . . but the presence of the Fuehrer and his confidence are a continual source of inspiration. For me, my stay here is like a fortnight of youth!'

He put down the phone and turned to Hanna, who was standing behind him. She leaned down and put her arms round him.

'Dear Hanna . . .' he said, 'how wrong I was to think this trip wasn't important. Now I see why the Fuehrer wanted me in Berlin! It was even worth losing my leg. It is only from here that you can get a clear picture.

Later that day there was yet another futile staff meeting. Von Greim was the only newcomer. The rest performed their actions like the familiar rite of a religious sect.

'For almost a week,' Krebs said, 'the population of Berlin have been living in cellars and in the corridors and passages of the Underground.'

Hitler interrupted sharply, 'in what sense do you mean "population"?'

'Women, the sick, boys under thirteen, old people over seventy, the mutilated – my Fuehrer.'

He waited for a reaction. Nothing happened. He went on, 'The hospitals and first aid posts in the Underground are overflowing with wounded. For days food and now even water have run out.'

'Pass on to the military situation, General Krebs,' Hitler rapped out. 'The question of civilians must take second place at a time like the present.'

Krebs had expected it. He continued with the catastrophic news in a matter-of-fact way. 'In Berlin, the

Hitler's pet dog, Blondi, was poisoned by his doctor

Top   Eva Braun *(right)* and her sister

Bottom   Hermann Goering was captured and committed suicide in 1946

Right   One of the few photographs of the elusive Martin Bormann

Hitler's 'wedding reception'; a scene from the film, *Hitler: The Last Ten Days*

Russians have attacked the Teltow Canal . . . our system of defence has been wiped out.'

Hitler's expression became a little grimmer than before. The officers looked dejectedly at one another.

'The Russians obviously intend to capture the bridges over the Ravel,' Krebs said.

'Where is General Weidling?' Hitler demanded. 'Why is he not present for the report?'

'He should be here at any moment, my Fuehrer.'

'And Wenck? What about Wenck? If he reached Ferch this morning, by now he *must* have covered the last six miles to Potsdam. He will have linked up with our troops down there!'

But there was no 'must' about anything.

'There has been no communication since this morning,' Krebs said soberly. 'The telephone cable and bunker radio are no longer in operation. We must wait for General Weidling.'

Hitler turned to von Greim. 'The Luftwaffe needs you in command. It is obvious that what they need is a new leader. If Wenck gets the necessary air cover, his breakthrough cannot fail.'

'We tried two take-offs this morning, but the fire from the enemy batteries was too fierce. We'll try again this evening.'

Hitler looked at Goebbels. 'Any news, Dr Goebbels, about the conflict between the Americans and Russians on the Elbe?'

'No further news, my Fuehrer. Allied censorship is obviously blocking every reference to it.'

'That's a good sign. It means the situation is serious. It's even possible they are already fighting. Inevitably they must. In their own interest, England and America must prevent the Russians from conquering Berlin. Once Stalin has Berlin in his grasp, he will never let it go. That should be clear even to the befuddled alcoholic brain of Churchill.'

Goebbels pulled a sheet of paper out of his pocket. 'I have prepared a leaflet to be distributed among the population and troops on the clash between the Russians and Americans, underlining the situation as extremely favourable to our cause.

But Hitler shook his head and pushed it away. Then he leaned over the maps again. 'The danger point is the Havel bridgeheads,' he announced. 'They are the only access to the city open to Wenck's army. They must be held at all costs.'

It was asking the impossible and everyone knew it. But no one was prepared for what followed.

'To ensure an unconditional resistance to the last drop of blood,' Hitler went on, straightening up and speaking to them as if he were addressing a public meeting. 'I order that the entire forces of the Hitler Youth, under Hitler Jugend Fuehrer Axmann, be concentrated to hold the Havel bridgeheads!'

Hoffmann looked aghast at the Fuehrer. None of the others spoke. Then after a moment's precautionary hesitation, Krebs said, 'But they're only children, my Fuehrer. They're full of fight and courage – true enough. But they aren't trained for fighting. It will be a massacre.'

TWENTY-THREE

'Many will die, I know,' Hitler went on, 'but millions of German soldiers have already died. The age one dies – that doesn't count when you die to gain time for your Fatherland. The valour of these fifteen and sixteen year old boys, dying in their thousands, is the most solid guarantee for Berlin holding out unflinchingly until the arrival of Wenck.'

No one agreed but not one of them opened his mouth. Hitler knew it and looked at them with contempt. 'Pass on my order to Hitler Jugend Fuehrer Axmann immediately. In fact I'll send General Fegelein directly with two cases of Iron Crosses for the boys who fight the most heroically . . .'

He paused, looking round for Fegelein. 'Where is General Fegelein?'

'I haven't seen him for two days, my Fuehrer,' said Hoffmann. Hitler glowered back and hissed, 'Have them find him. And now, gentlemen, we can adjourn this meeting until the first news reaches us of Wenck's Army on the march.'

But before he had time to get to his feet, the door opened and a general in battle-worn uniform was led in, his face looking haggard, exhausted and filthy. He came to attention. 'General Weidling, Military Commander of Berlin, reporting . . . Heil, my Fuehrer!'

Hitler returned his salute and looked at him, his eyes bright with hope. 'News of Wenck's army?'

'Yes, my Fuehrer. General Wenck informed me half an hour ago that he has been attacked on both flanks by the Russians, who are advancing on his position, encircling him.'

TWENTY-FOUR

It was as if the last light of hope had been extinguished. Hitler's head and hands began to shake badly, but it was the only visible reaction.

His eyes bored into General Weidling, who carried on

stoically. 'Wenck's army, my Fuehrer, is took weak to hold the area they have captured south of Potsdam. They cannot hope to penetrate into the centre of Berlin. Yet the forces of the city garrison are still strong enough to bring off a sortie and join up with Wenck.'

'My Fuehrer, I personally guarantee to conduct you safely out of Berlin. In doing so we shall be able to prevent the sacred capital of the Reich from becoming the battleground for the final death struggle.'

Hitler said, 'Have we ever met before, General?'

'Yes, my Fuehrer. A year ago . . . you conferred a decoration on me.'

Hitler stared at him for a full minute, then he turned to Krebs, 'I confirm my orders, General Krebs!'

'Does that apply to the orders for – the Hitler Youth?'

Hitler tore into him, his eyes flashing. 'You have no faith in the young, General Krebs . . . but I have! Those boys will save Berlin and the honour of Germany with their lives. Thank you, gentlemen . . .'

They turned and left, making way for von Greim to be carried out. In a few moments Hitler was left alone.

He looked at the door a long time as if to make sure that there was nobody there. Then his face slowly relaxed into bewilderment, depression and dejection. His eyes lost their mad brilliance and faded into an infinite sadness. Very slowly he rested his elbows on the table and dropped his head into his hands. It was the posture of a gambler who has been wiped into oblivion at the very last throw.

TWENTY-FIVE

Late in the evening, Hitler took his dog for her walk round the corridors of the Bunker. Despite the fact that everyone he met saluted or made some other gesture of acknowledgement, his solitude was absolute.

He reached the door of the Goebbels' apartment, knocked and went inside. Magda and her children were there, having tea. Magda was overjoyed at the honour and the children immediately stood to attention.

'Heil, my Fuehrer!' Hitler smiled at them.

'My Fuehrer! What a surprise! What an honour!' Magda exclaimed.

'Don't let me disturb you,' Hitler said, and let Blondi off her leash. 'Please, all of you, sit down.'

They all settled down again, and Hitler ordered his dog to sit. Blondi obediently went to a corner of the room.

'Is everything in order here, Magda?' Hitler enquired, like an affable sergeant doing his rounds. 'Ventilators working as they should? Excellent! . . . what's that you're drinking, Helga? Chocolate? Come – sit on my lap.'

Helga, a pretty little girl with shining blonde hair, traipsed across and sat awkwardly on his lap, and in so doing, spilled hot chocolate on the Fuehrer's trousers. Magda was horrified.

'Helga!' she yelled, and then snatching up a cloth, she daubed at the stain. 'My Fuehrer! I cannot say how sorry I am . . .'

Helga began to cry. Hitler held up his hand. 'It's nothing. She didn't mean any harm, did you, little Helga?' The child stopped crying and shook her head vehemently. 'Really, Magda, it's nothing at all – please forget about it.'

Helmut, one of Goebbels' sons, came and stood beside his mother carrying a bowl of hot water. 'Ah! Helmut!' Hitler said with a smile. 'Always the efficient one! One of these days, my boy, as I've told you before, you'll make a marvellous soldier.'

By this time another of the children had brought the Fuehrer a cup of tea. He lifted the cup in the gesture of a toast. 'Well, my god-children, I drink to you all . . . to health and happiness for the rest of your days.'

'Thank you, my Fuehrer,' some of them began, but a heavy shell overhead drowned their words. One or two of the children were disturbed and couldn't help looking uneasy. But Hitler went on beaming benevolently at them all. Magda, who had recovered from her little calamity, was enraptured.

That night in Hitler's study, the court was relaxing as usual round a table laden with cakes and champagne. Hitler was exercising his normal monopoly on the conversation. 'However, I have no intention of imposing conditions on anybody,' he spoke calmly and easily. 'I have always respected the desires and wishes of my collaborators and if any of you are not in agreement, then you are at liberty to say so.'

Goebbels got in first. 'Allow me to speak on behalf of my wife and myself. Our doubts only concern the way . . . on how to do it . . . not what we are going to do . . .'

'And your children?' Hitler asked solicitously.

'We cannot abandon them in a moment like this,' Magda said. 'What point would their lives have for them now? To leave them in a world without you, my Fuehrer, is like ordering them to live in hell . . . on an earth without sunshine.'

Hitler considered this for a moment. 'You're right – all too right – it's the kindest thing to do.'

Eva Braun said anxiously, 'You must absolutely try and do it in a way they won't really notice.'

'Cyanide, Fraulein Braun,' Hitler observed in a businesslike way, 'three seconds and everything is over. Isn't that correct, Dr Stumpfegger?'

The doctor was pouring himself a drink and being thoroughly sociable.

'Yes, indeed . . . except for the extremely rare cases of biological rejection or mithridatism.'

This was meaningless to Eva. For a fleeting moment she looked puzzled but tried not to give herself away. But Hitler noticed, and instead of helping, simply compounded her confusion.

'Which reminds me, Eva . . . you are right. I shall have to stop taking those pills of Dr Morell's. I don't want to risk a repetition in my own case of what happened to Mithridatus, the famous King of Pontus.'

Eva was completely lost, and Hitler relished her embarrassment. 'He kept taking small doses of poison to build up his resistance. Well it did. In order to kill him they had to resort to God knows what in the end . . .'

There were one or two sycophantic smiles. Bormann said to Goebbels in a voice deep with emotion: 'Our Fuehrer's erudition really is extraordinary.'

Von Greim sat in his new and flamboyant uniform, his leg still resting on a chair. He leaned forward and announced dramatically, 'Fraulein Hanna and I thought of jumping out of an aeroplane over Berlin, but we felt that was a bit theatrical so we changed our minds.'

'General von Greim and I shall die in each other's arms,' said Hanna.

Eva was entranced. 'How noble! That's beautiful, Fraulein Hanna . . . you mean – simply hold on to each other and . . . and . . .'

'Of course not, Fraulein Braun. We shall be holding a hand grenade between us. Then we shall take out the pin . . .'

'Magnificent!' Hitler said with admiration. 'You understand, Fraulein Braun?'

'Yes,' Eva was doubtful, 'but I should be afraid of just being disfigured forever after. Anyway, I'd like a quieter death than that.'

Hanna raised an eyebrow and exchanged a look of

contempt with Magda Goebbels. She was about to cap Eva's remark when Hitler patted Eva's hand and said, 'Ah yes . . . charmingly feminine.'

'It's been years since I've had time to be charmingly feminine,' Hanna said in a savage undertone.

'We still haven't had the opinion of our good Fraulein Manzialy.' Hitler looked up at her while she passed round the tea.

She smiled. 'If those pig-faced Russians come here, I'll turn on the gas and die at my battle station, in the kitchen.'

'I'll shoot!' Fraulein Junge swore, 'I'll shoot them! I'll kill a whole bunch of them first before I kill myself.'

'I'm told the best place to shoot oneself is in the mouth,' Frau Christian remarked helpfully.

'But then I couldn't die with the Fuehrer's name on my lips.'

'That's true . . . the heart, then.'

'The heart is too unsafe,' Hitler spoke with authority. 'Your hand only has to tremble while you press the trigger and the shot could go wide.'

'Which is why,' said General Burgdorf, 'I shall express my loyalty by finding death in battle, my Fuehrer. When the time comes . . .'

'I don't agree, General. You run the risk of being taken prisoner, tortured and forced to betray your oath.'

'Like Paulus at Stalingrad,' Bormann said.

'I can't bear to think of that,' Hitler said sorrowfully. 'A man who besmirched the heroism of so many others . . . He could have achieved national immortality by killing himself. Instead, he chose to go to Moscow. And to think I had only just made him a Feldmarschall!'

He pulled himself out of this unpleasant train of thought. 'What about you, Bormann?'

Bormann gave a twisted smile.

'It's something I keep thinking about over and over

again. I am wavering between two completely different ways . . . either drowning myself in the Spree – simple but a bit common – or throwing myself on to one of my men's bayonets.'

'Like Nero.'

Bormann laughed, a little uncomfortably. 'History holds no secrets for you, my Fuehrer.'

He was answered by a quick smirk of self-satisfaction. Then Hitler's face clouded over. 'What about Fegelein?' he asked. 'Where's Fegelein? I am very curious to know if he has decided to die . . . and how. He hasn't been seen for the last two days.'

He turned peremptorily to Bormann. 'Send for the Chief of the Security Forces – Hoegl!'

Everyone watched Bormann as he left the room, except the Fuehrer, who cut himself another slice of chocolate cake.

TWENTY-SIX

The door closed behind Bormann and Eva asked, 'And what about you, my Fuehrer? What have you decided?'

He sat back drumming his fingertips together. It was as if he was considering the question for the first time.

'For physical reasons,' he began, 'it won't be possible for me to fight. And even if I were thoroughly fit, I still wouldn't fight. I cannot risk being wounded and falling into the hands of the enemy. That is why I shall kill myself.'

There was a subdued gasp of horror.

'I shall simply use a combination of different methods,' Hitler went on. 'Dr Stumpfegger's cyanide. My pistol and Guensche's pistol. Finally, my driver Kempka will have the task of pouring petrol over my corpse and setting it on fire.'

Goebbels said to his wife, 'That's a good idea – the petrol. After we've poisoned the children, Magda, we'd better follow the same course.'

'The only thing I'm afraid of, my dear Goebbels,' Hitler remarked, 'is that you may have trouble finding enough petrol.'

He smiled knowingly at Eva. 'I've had some put aside for myself, and eventually for you, Fraulein Braun.'

'Thank you, my Fuehrer.'

'There seems to be a shortage of cyanide and petrol in the bunker. It's easier to find whipped cream these days, isn't it, Frau Manzialy?' he said, and took yet another elaborate confection.

There was an abrupt knock at the door, and an aide entered followed by Hoegl, a sinister figure in the uniform of the SS. Hoegl stamped to attention. Everyone else went quiet. Hitler kept them waiting. He bit into his cake, savoured it and then suddenly shouted at Hoegl, 'General Fegelein has been absent without leave! I order you to search for him and bring him here immediately!' Hoegl saluted and was about to go when a possible difficulty occurred to him. 'But what if he has crossed the Russian line, my Fuehrer? His house lies in a part of the city already occupied.'

'Captain Hoffmann will go with you. He knows the places where he can get through. I want General Fegelein brought back here instantly. That is an order! And, of course, you will answer for it with your life.'

Hoegl saluted again and strode out of the room. Hitler turned back to the others with a sociable smile. 'It would be a pity if Fegelein chose an execution squad as a means of suicide . . . in order to prove his loyalty.'

The hunt for General Fegelein began. The Fuehrer was

right: Hoffmann did know his way around. He led Hoegl and twenty SS guards through the dark, ruined streets, over and round great mounds of rubble, past the gaunt skeletons of buildings which had once been the pride of the glorious Third Reich; a shadowy Pompeii, lit only by the flashes of the encircling gunfire.

Eventually they found the apartment. It was in pitch darkness. Hoffmann hammered on the door but there was no response. Across what was left of the street the SS waited, crouching in doorways and at corners, watching intently for any sign of life.

Hoffmann continued to pound on the door. After a very long wait, it opened and a youngish, pretty, frail-looking woman appeared, clutching a man's bathrobe around her naked body.

She was making a brave effort to behave naturally. When she spoke, her voice had a noticeable but indefinite foreign accent.

'Who are you looking for, Captain?'

'General Fegelein,' Hoffmann said curtly.

The woman did not know what to do.

'Really . . . I don't know if . . .'

Her defences crumbled and Fegelein himself appeared and stood behind her in the doorway. He, too, was in a dressing gown which he was pulling hastily around himself. He was perfectly calm when he spoke. in no way embarrassed.

'All right, Elsa.'

Hoffmann saluted. 'Heil Hitler!'

Fegelein gave him a cheerful grin and put out his hand. 'We can forget the formalities now, Hoffmann.' He took Hoffmann confidentially by the arm and led him inside. The woman watched them anxiously. Fegelein smiled re-assuringly at her, 'The Captain is an old friend, Elsa. No trouble. I'm sorry, Hoffmann,' he went on steering him through into an elegant bedroom with an unmade bed, 'I hope you don't mind finding me in this rather unorthodox way, but I've had a bit of a cold the past couple of days.'

Hoffmann was amazed by this display of coolness. Fegelein gave him a knowing smile. 'We were getting some rest, Elsa and I . . . anyway now you're in, make yourself at home. I'll put on some clothes, but I'm not going to stand on ceremony with you. I could see all along you were certainly no fool.' Fegelein put on a pair of civilian trousers.

'General Fegelein, I have the Fuehrer's personal orders to bring you back to the Bunker with me.'

'Come, come, Hoffmann!' Fegelein said; he was amused. 'Everything is lost by now, and you know it as well as I do. So take off your uniform and stop playing the fool. I'll give you a suit of mine and you can come away with me . . .'

'That is not what I am here for, General Fegelein.'

Fegelein finished buttoning up his trousers. 'There's not one chance in a million of getting out of that bunker alive. The Russkys will crucify us. If he wants to die, he's perfectly free to do it. He has his accounts to settle with history. But as for us . . . you and me . . . we've only ourselves to settle with.'

For a moment Fegelein's nerve struck Hoffmann dumb. He recovered quickly. 'You are right, General Fegelein. We only have to settle accounts with ourselves. But do you think you can do that by an act of cowardice?' He paused. Fegelein looked at him in surprise. 'You have received a lot from the Fuehrer and from National Socialism,' Hoffmann went on, 'you've cried "Traitor" at others. You've executed orders you know to be cruel. You can't blot it all out, now, at the last moment, just by putting on a civilian jacket and a pair of trousers – and then bolting.' He paused again and then stood at attention. 'I must ask you to follow me to the Bunker.'

The woman listened to them in growing panic. Fegelein, however, simply laughed. 'My dear Hoffmann, I haven't the slightest intention of following you.'

While he laughed he also moved a little closer towards a pistol which lay on the dressing-table.

'You don't seem to understand, General Fegelein. Outside SS Standartenfuehrer Hoegl has twenty men watching the house. You have no means of escape.'

The colour drained from Fegelein's face and, watching him, the woman burst into tears. Fegelein turned on her in a fury. 'Stop that blubbering and go into the other room! Go on! Get out of here!'

Fegelein turned back to Hoffmann as the woman disappeared in a flood of tears. 'Will you allow me to make a phone call, Captain? Though I'm afraid it won't be of the slightest use . . .' Hoffmann stood aside and Fegelein went past him to the telephone which was on a side table. He dialled, but his hand had begun to shake . . .

'Fraulein Braun, please . . . her brother-in-law, General Fegelein.'

While Fegelein waited, he stared at Hoffmann with cold, expressionless eyes. Elsa was still crying in the next room, and outside the almost continuous fury of the Russian shellfire crashed and pounded into the city. Eva Braun came onto the line.

'Hallo, Eva.' Fegelein was striving to sound calm and matter-of-fact. 'It's Hermann . . . in Berlin, of course . . there must be some misunderstanding . . . there are some men here who have come to arrest me . . . please, you must speak to the Fuehrer.'

Fegelein darted, a sudden, scared look at the door behind which Elsa was crying and then went on, his voice low and his hand cupped round the mouthpiece, 'You know how I love your sister . . . and my child's waiting to be born any day now . . .'

Even across the room, Hoffmann could hear Eva's

voice strident with anger. 'You can't do this to Gretl and me . . . you can't betray the Fuehrer!'

'You know I'd do *anything* for the Fuehrer,' Fegelein said, avoiding Hoffmann's stare, 'but wanting to be with my wife and child has nothing to do with betraying . . .'

At that moment the outer door crashed open and SS Standartenfuehrer Hoegl followed by two SS guards, burst into the room. Hoegl did not wait to be asked to speak. 'Hurry up, Herr General. We have no more time. Every minute the situation gets more dangerous. Come . . . now!'

General Fegelein went pale. His face broke out in a sweat as he looked first at Hoegl, then at Hoffmann. He put the receiver down slowly without saying another word, picked up his uniform jacket and then walked out behind Hoegl and the guards, his head bent. With a last look round the room, Hoffmann followed closing the door quietly behind him and shutting out forever the sound of Elsa's crying.

TWENTY-SEVEN

'I swear to you, my Fuehrer, I never wanted to betray you . . . the only reason I went home was to get some civilian clothes which would allow me to get across the lines without being noticed . . . then I caught a bad cold, my Fuehrer. My sole intention was – and is, if you will permit it, to join the army of Wenck.'

General Fegelein of the SS was pleading for his life. He wore his General's jacket over a pair of ill-cut civilian trousers. A guard stood on either side of him with Hoegl behind, his pistol drawn. Hitler stared at Fegelein with an expression of contempt. 'You must believe me, my Fuehrer. If I'd wanted to desert, I'd have gone to some little hotel or a neighbour's house . . . not to my own apartment. I even got hold of one of those foreign-labour women to help me across the lines more easily. She speaks a bit of Russian, you see . . .' It was a brave performance, but it was in danger of petering out completely in the atmosphere of freezing scorn.

He struggled on. 'You see, I wanted to be personally sure that Wenck was carrying out his orders, and that he wasn't proving to be a traitor . . . like Steiner and all the others in the Army . . . then I was going to come back to Berlin with the Twelfth Army and fight all the way to the Bunker . . . to save you, my Fuehrer . . . and . . . and all the others . . .'

The pitiless silence finally crushed him.

'Degrade him.' The words had a flat finality about them.

The two guards turned, and with ill-disguised relish began to rip off the insignia of rank and the decorations. Hitler watched poker-faced as the ex-General's jacket was turned into a tattered mess.

'Hold him under arrest until he is tried.'

Fegelein was removed. Quietly and without ostentation, everyone who had been watching melted out of the room. Hitler sat alone. His eyes glistened with tears, his face was stony with despair and disillusionment.

Later that night, the thirty feet of concrete above them were being repeatedly struck by shells and bombs. The whole place shook as if a spasmodic earthquake were in progress. The ventilators had stopped working and a thick white powder filled the rooms.

The physical and emotional strain to which they were subjected had begun to attack the spirit of all but the most insane. The majority of them realised that the end could not be far away, but they faced it with a spirit of recklessness induced by the voracious consumption of the Bunker liquor stocks.

111

In one room after another, SS guards, officers, service women, medical orderlies and nurses were mixing all the expensive wines and liqueurs they could lay their hands on. Exotic foodstuffs, originally pillaged from cities like Paris and Strasbourg, were mixed up with ordinary rations in a grotesque feast, as though oblivion could be sought through one last, monstrous appeasement of the appetite.

In the officers' mess room, Bormann, Krebs and Burgdorf had all had so much to eat and drink that they could scarcely move. Their liquor intake had also stripped them of their inhibitions; their discretion and circumspection, their caution bred of long years of self-preservation, had all vanished.

Slumped into a chair, Bormann shouted at Burgdorf, 'It's true . . . absolutely true and history will confirm it word for word . . .' He lost the thread of his thought, '. . . word for word.'

Burgdorf grunted.

'The army of the Reich,' Bormann slurred on, 'is composed of traitors, fuckers, cowards, degenerates . . . they have all ruined our Fuehrer . . . the Party . . . everybody . . . everybody . . .'

His voice choked into silence as Hoffmann appeared at the door. Hoffmann was not drunk, and he could scarcely believe his eyes. He looked at his senior officers and his stomach turned over in disgust. At this moment, Burgdorf managed to comprehend what Bormann had been saying; he staggered up out of his seat, threw his glass against the concrete wall of the Bunker and started to scream in a poor imitation of the Fuehrer, 'Shut up! Shut up! You give me a pain in the arse, all of you. For the last nine months I've been trying to harmonise the Army and the Party – why? Out of pure idealism, that's why.'

He paused, swaying unsteadily. 'And now, my old friends and fellow officers don't greet me any more . . .

I've done all that is possible to break down the Party leaders' suspicions of the Army . . . I was even called a traitor by my fellow officers of the General Staff . . . but when I hear the sort of bullshit that lunatic is yelling,' he jabbed a finger roughly in the direction of Bormann's face, 'I can only say that I've been a prick . . . they were right to insult me, call me a traitor . . . my idealism was false . . . not even that, it was just silly and half-witted . . . the idealism of a real prick against the idiotic arrogance of the Party!'

He ran out of words and dropped down in dejection. Hoffmann looked on, still unable to believe his eyes. Bormann appeared not to have heard or, if he had, not to have taken in the meaning. Krebs said to Burgdorf, 'Leave him alone . . . leave him alone . . . please . . .' His voice, too, was thick, and sounded on the point of tears. 'Please, I beg of you . . . leave our dear Comrade Bormann alone . . .'

He wrung his hands ineffectually as Burgdorf shook his head and worked himself up for a further drunken harangue. 'No, no, no . . . for once in a while, I've got to let it all come tumbling out . . . my dear Hans . . . another twenty-four hours and it'll probably be too late . . . our young officers there, like him,' he pointed at Hoffmann, 'our young officers have fought with faith and enthusiasm which are unique in the history of the world . . . hundreds of thousands have gone to their death smiling . . . and for what? For their beloved German fatherland? For our future? For a greater, more civilised Germany? No! No!'

He staggered over to Hoffmann and bellowed into his face, 'The ones like you who are dead . . . do you know why their died, Captain? They died for them . . .' he pointed to the half-slumbering Bormann. 'You will all die to make them rich, to quench their thirst for power . . . They've been waving the flags and beating the drums for a cause none of them intended to honour . . . but they forced millions of you to shed your blood on all the battlefields of Europe . . . a whole generation wiped out . . .'

He stumbled over to Bormann. 'They died in their millions . . . and you Party leaders, you've got your hands on the people's heritage . . . you've been guzzling it all from an inexhaustible feed box. You've piled up your wealth, robbed estates, built palaces, rotted yourselves with vice . . . cheated honest people. You have dragged our morals, our faith, our spirit through the mud . . . human beings are only the grist of your insatiable thirst for power. You have rubbed out centuries of culture – the civilisation of our people . . .'

He dropped to his knees as if struck by lightning, his head against the wall. He stayed there, tears gushing down his cheeks. Instinctively Hoffmann went to help him, bending down to try and lift him. But Burgdorf pushed him roughly aside and muttered, 'Go on, get away from me, Captain . . . go and die for that thieving swine . . .'

Hoffmann straightened up. He was dazed. Nothing made sense any more. He looked at Bormann who had hoisted himself out of his armchair and was pouring himself a huge glass of brandy.

'My dear Burgdorf . . .' Bormann began, 'You mustn't confuse . . . you mustn't confuse . . . you mustn't confuse . . . No, definitely, you mustn't confuse . . .' He tailed off, trying in vain to remember what he was going to say.

'The *others* might have got rich, yes, but I am . . . innocent . . . innocent . . . innocent. Completely and utterly innocent. I swear by all that I hold most sacred . . .' He lifted the full glass and began to tilt it towards his mouth. The brandy ran off his lips and splashed his uniform. 'Your health, my very dear friend, my dearest friend . . .'

Krebs came up alongside and helped him to hold his glass. His coordination was equally poor. 'No, no, my dear Bormann,' Krebs said, carefully enunciating his words, 'you mustn't swear by all you hold sacred . . . too dangerous . . .' He shook his head, 'You bought a big estate in Mecklenburg . . . and an even bigger one in Upper Bavaria. You own half of Berchtesgaden . . . you even bought the Fuehrer's house in Linz and transformed it – transformed it into a museum where people pay to go in . . . you are building a villa on Chiemsee . . . you mustn't swear by all you hold sacred . . . you really mustn't . . . your wife could die . . . or one of your children . . . or both . . . Don't you think so, Hoffmann?'

TWENTY-EIGHT

The next morning – 28 April 1945 – Hitler left his study with Goebbels, Hanna Reitsch and Eva Braun and picked his way over the massive recumbent bodies of Krebs, Burgdorf and Bormann, who were all heavily asleep and snoring, sprawled in their armchairs.

The Fuehrer ignored them, and he ignored the stale air, heavy with the fumes of the previous night's drinking and smoking. He was petulant and querulous.

'It really is infuriating that connections are cut off. What a joy it would be to follow the conflict between the Russians and the Americans step by step . . . I wonder which of them will get in touch with me first: the Russian bear or that drunkard Churchill.'

'Perhaps Truman,' said Goebbels, 'unless the Jews refuse to allow him.'

They all laughed at this witty joke and, turning a corner, came across a skinny boy of fourteen, leaning against the corridor wall wearing a dirty uniform several sizes too large for him. He was clearly dazed from the shock of battle and terrified at finding himself in the

Fuehrerbunker. He forced himself to attention in an effort to control his fear and looked in panic from Hitler's grey, hollow face with its haunted stare to Goebbels, who said to the Fuehrer, 'This is the boy I told you about. He blew up a Stalin tank single-handed.'

'There's a hero for you, ladies,' smiled Hitler thinly, and turning to an attendant following him with a box of Iron Crosses, picked out one and pinned it to the boy's shirt. In doing so, he realised how frail the boy was, and was momentarily touched. He rested his hand on the boy's head. 'You're a good soldier,' he said, almost as if he were speaking to himself. Then, abruptly, he pulled himself together and asked, 'Is the front holding?'

'I think so,' the boy replied timidly. 'The losses are heavy. They say over five thousand in the last three days . . .'

Hitler stared at the boy for a moment or so and then walked away. The boy was left gazing after him and as one of the last adjutants passed, he asked in a small voice, 'Who was that gentleman, Herr Major?'

'What? . . . Didn't you recognise him? That was the Fuehrer.'

For a brief moment the boy's face lit up – then it crumpled, and tears of regret filled his eyes, regret at an opportunity lost forever.

There was a sinister development later in the day. Goebbels' adjutant rushed into the mess room where Bormann, Goebbels and Krebs sat together and handed them a despatch which had just been picked up from Reuters.

Bormann read it. 'Attempted peace negotiations initiated by Heinrich Himmler with the British and American forces through the mediation of Swedish Count Folke Bernadotte have failed. The Prime Minister, Mr Winston Churchill, has declared that no attempt at a negotiated peace will be taken into consideration. Only unconditional surrender to the three allied powers will be accepted as the basis for an armistice.'

Eventually Goebbels cleared his throat and said, 'Somebody will have to tell the Fuehrer . . .'

'Nobody could find the right words better than you, Dr Goebbels.'

'I don't think so, Herr Bormann . . . I think under the circumstances, you are the proper person . . . you know the Fuehrer so well.'

'I don't agree.' Bormann shook his head and looked at Krebs. 'To my mind, General Krebs, it is up to you . . .'

'*Me*?' Krebs replied, quite unable to disguise the panic gripping his guts, 'why *me*? This isn't a military question. Therefore it has nothing whatever to do with me.'

Goebbels turned to his adjutant. 'Lorenz – you brought this here – simply take it to the Fuehrer and hand it to him.'

But Lorenz was sweating with fear. 'Dr Goebbels . . . I really . . . I have very little personal contact with the Fuehrer.'

'The less you've had the better in a circumstance of this kind.'

But as he said it, his eyes wandered across the room and he added abruptly, 'Wait – I think I have an even simpler idea.'

Goebbels limped off across the room towards a small group of officers who were being served sandwiches by the old footman who had once been in charge of the registration book in the upper Chancellery. From behind the door of Hitler's study came the sound of his favourite record – *Die Fledermaus*. Goebbels drew the footman to one side, gave him the message, folded so he could not read it and instructed him on what to do. The old man was delighted.

'Thank you, Dr Goebbels. It is an honour for me to carry out such a commission.'

'The news it carries is top secret, remember.'

'Rely upon me, Your Excellency. I shall take it in at once.' He shook his head smiling in pleasure. 'This is a great moment in my life.'

He put down his tray and hurried across to the study door. Goebbels rejoined the other three and they all watched the old man. He knocked on the door and waited until he was told to come in. He opened the door, went through, and closed it behind him.

'Herr Bormann,' said Goebbels, 'may I have a word with you?'

TWENTY-NINE

The door to Hitler's study remained closed a long time. The anteroom was filling up. More and more people came in to try and check up on the rumours that a crisis had occurred. The buzz of hushed talk increased, together with the sense of anxiety and fear.

The music from *Die Fledermaus* stopped abruptly. Then with a crash the study door was wrenched open and Eva Braun ran out crying. She pushed through the mob around the door as though she neither saw them nor cared who they were. She was distraught. Sobbing hysterically she rushed headlong down the corridors to Magda Goebbels' room.

Hanna Reitsch was with Frau Goebbels and both women looked up in some astonishment as Eva Braun threw herself wildly on to the bed, buried her face in a pillow and shrieked, 'It's Himmler! They've all betrayed him! Now Himmler too! They've all abandoned the Fuehrer!'

She was choked with sobbing. 'Poor, poor Adolf . . .' she cried, 'he *must* live . . . the others can die . . . all the others . . . all of them but he . . . he must live.'

In the Fuhrer's study the mainstream of the crisis raged on like an alpine torrent. Hitler's pasty complexion had become a reddish-purple. His fury had attained new heights; nothing could contain his wrath.

'He was a nobody!' Hitler screamed, 'Nobody! Everything he ever had he got from me! That swine Goering – I expected *him* to betray me one day . . . a besotted drug-addict will do anything in the end. But Himmler! My faithful Heinrich. He owed everything to me, everything! I hauled him out of the mud! I believed in him! For me he became the symbol of German loyalty – and now he has plunged a dagger in my back . . .'

Goebbels and Bormann, who had been called in to hear the news, said nothing. It was elementary wisdom since anything they said at such a moment could all too easily be turned against them.

'Why? Why did Himmler betray me? Why did Fegelein before him – Goering, Rommel, Kluge and all the others?' The voice was bewildered, agonised. He searched his thoughts for an answer and said triumphantly, 'I know why. Because no ordinary man can follow me to reach my heights . . . not even Speer . . . and Speer is a genius too . . . but not a genius great enough to understand *my* genius . . .'

He took a deep breath and continued. 'I am too great for the time we live in, for this pedestrian humanity of to-day. Sometimes I wonder whether destiny was not mistaken in placing the German people in my hands . . . perhaps the English would have understood me better . . . they are nordic aryans too and they have never had traitors . . . under that hopeless alcoholic Churchill they are doomed of course – but if *I* could have taken them in hand, I would have led them to greatness and glory and made the British Empire master of the world for one thousand years.'

He paused again, relishing and revisualising the scene.

Then with deep sadness, he said 'The German people are a nation of whores . . . none of them deserve me . . . they haven't allowed me to do what I wanted to do for them, so they must be punished and it is destiny which will punish them . . . And I, who could have been destiny's instrument to give the Germans world fame, will be the instrument of their chastisement. Because – when I am here no more, no German will be able to bear the disgrace and the grief of my loss. They shall live in misery, in the blackest remorse and poverty for the next hundred years. Only in a hundred years' time, perhaps, a genius will appear to redeem them and offer them a chance of salvation. He will take me as his model, use my ideas and follow the path that I have charted . . .' Hitler slumped back, a hunched and shrunken figure staring hungrily out into space.

'But perhaps there is some good in all this, my Fuehrer,' Bormann suggested, hesitantly. 'Now that all the traitors are unmasked, we finally know whom we can really count on.'

Hitler looked at him absently for a second or two and then suddenly his mood changed again. He spoke savagely, his voice was pitiless and aggressive. 'Now I understand that miserable worm Fegelein . . . I'm sure he was in this with Himmler . . . part of an SS plot to assassinate me and sell my body to the Allies.'

He picked up the telephone. 'I want the Chief of the Gestapo, Muller, over here immediately . . . he is? Send him in.'

He put back the phone and waited in silence, his eyes consumed with hatred and the desire for vengeance. The Chief of the Gestapo was not long in coming.

'Heil, my Fuehrer!'

Hitler acknowledged the salute and then said mercilessly, 'Muller! Interrogate Fegelein . . . he was in league with Himmler. He was part of an SS plot to assasinate me and sell my corpse to the Allies. I want this confession without delay.'

'Yes, my Fuehrer.'

'Then shoot him!'

The Chief of the Gestapo saluted again and left the room. His expression was exultant.

THIRTY

It had been a bad day for Eva. By evening she felt she had spent most of her waking hours crying. She was still hiding her face in her hands so that the Fuehrer couldn't see her tear-stained cheeks. Hitler stood beside her with a face of stone.

'Fegelein is a murderer. There must be no pity for him. Remember Mussolini and Ciano. Ciano was his son-in-law. Yet when I asked for him to be shot, Mussolini did so without a scruple.'

'You are the Fuehrer,' Eva sobbed. 'Family considerations don't count. Whatever you decide is right . . .'

Hitler for once showed some emotion for her. He bent over her heaving body and tried to hold her close to him and to part her hands from her face. But Eva resisted, shaking her head.

'No, Adolf . . . please . . . don't look at me now. I'm so ugly . . . my eyes are all swollen and red . . . let me pull myself together . . . I never want you to see me ugly.'

Shells were falling all round the Bunker. Hoffmann went to get some air, standing in the shelter of the Bunker doorway. He watched the fountains of earth and plants which each new shell threw up as it smashed into the Chancellery grounds. Just as he thought he could not bear to watch it any longer, he saw a girl dressed in the Women's Auxiliary uniform come running through the craters.

'Where do you think you're going?' Hoffmann asked her, as he grabbed her and dragged her into the doorway.

'Volkssturm Auxiliary Hilde Lange . . . Heil Hitler!'

Hoffmann did not bother to answer her salute. 'What do you want here?'

'The Iron Crosses for the Hitler Youth. General Axmann sent me to get them.'

There was a thin scream as a shell fell nearby and exploded. Hoffmann and the girl threw themselves down and then dragged themselves shakily to their feet.

Hoffmann said sarcastically, 'You have the necessary forms in triplicate?'

Hilde took him seriously. 'Forms? General Axmann didn't give be any forms.'

'Ah!' He looked at her torn uniform, her straw blonde hair, and her adolescent face.

'Do you really think forms are necessary, Captain?' the girl said with a gesture of her head at the wreckage around them.

Hoffmann smiled. 'Stay in the doorway. I'll see what I can do.'

Hoffmann went down into the Bunker. The girl turned and looked around. She stooped over a scrap of flowerbed which had remained intact and bent down to pick a flower, then quickly straightened up as she heard shouting and the clatter of feet coming up the bunker steps.

Fegelein was being led out of the Bunker in handcuffs. He had been worked over by the Gestapo guards. Four of them stood round him and shoved him forward towards the back wall of the Chancellery. Bruised, bleeding and not fully conscious, Fegelein knew only that he was going to be shot.

The girl watched, the flowers still in her hand. Behind

Fegelein two more SS guards dragged out the old footman. He too was in handcuffs, struggling furiously, and weeping piteously. 'What's happening? Why? What have I done? What for? . . . I haven't done anything.'

The guards pushed Fegelein and the old man against the wall and hastily arranged themselves into a firing line. Without warning they heard the scream of another shell and a second later there was a massive explosion which raised a sea of earth from the centre of the garden. The squad of executioners and their two victims all threw themselves onto the ground.

It was the weirdest scene Hilde had seen in her whole life. The guards got to their feet, retrieved their weapons, and pushed Fegelein and the footman back against the wall. Then they opened fire. Fegelein fell without a sound. The old man gave a last, whimpering cry and died without knowing why.

Hilde was trembling when the SS threw the bodies into a bomb crater and went back into the Bunker.

'Here you are,' Hoffmann said and gave her two boxes covered in red Moroccan leather. 'There are a hundred first class and thirty second class. You'll have to manage with these as best you can.'

She smiled briefly and took the boxes. Hoffmann offered her a packet of cigarettes. 'Are these any use?'

Hilde put her hand out to take one.

'Take the packet.' He pulled two more packets out of his pocket. 'Take these too.'

'Thanks. Don't you smoke?'

'Hardly ever . . .' he smiled. 'Good luck.'

'The same to you, Herr Captain . . .'

She hesitated, wanting to ask him about the executions, and turned to look at the pock-marked wall. But then with a little shrug of her shoulders and a smile she turned and left . . .

Down in Hitler's study Feldmarschall von Greim, supported by an SS guard, was given his orders by the Fuehrer. Hitler was cold and worn out but was still fired by rage and an implacable hatred for the traitors. Bormann and Goebbels sat with him. Magda and Eva were writing letters at the desk.

'Once you have arrived safely at the seat of your command, every aircraft must be used to destroy the Russian tanks advancing on the Bunker.' Hitler's voice was shrill and slightly out of control once more.

He clenched his fists. 'We must gain time and allow the Allies to fight it out among themselves.' Then he switched to another tack. 'The moment you reach staff headquarters, have Himmler arrested . . . In no case – never – must a traitor succeed me as Fuehrer.'

Chief of the Gestapo Muller came in. 'Heil, my Fuehrer! Your orders have been carried out. General Fegelein has been executed.'

Hitler was not interested. He continued to talk to von Greim, looking him in the eye. 'I have complete faith in you, Feldmarschall. Act as you see fit. Decide for yourself what to do about Himmler. But understand, I do not want him to take my place. A traitor like that must be crushed and swept from the face of the earth.'

Hanna Reitsch looked up at Hitler and her eyes were brimming with tears. 'But why – why, my Fuehrer? Why won't you allow us to stay here at your side?'

Hitler looked straight through her. 'Von Greim, a traitor has no right to be my successor. The responsibility that Himmler does not do so is yours.'

General Christian interrupted. 'Herr Feldmarschall, the plane is waiting beneath the Victory Column with its engines running.' The walls of the Bunker shook with another heavy explosion. Magda and Eva hastily sealed their letters, stood up and gave them to Hanna Reitsch.

'Mine is for my son, Harold,' said Magda. 'I'm counting on you, Hanna.'

'And this is for my family,' said Eva. 'Please see that it gets to Munich.'

Hanna took the letters mechanically and pocketed them. She was crying without restraint, her eyes fixed on Hitler, though he himself appeared to be oblivious of her.

THIRTY-ONE

The plane succeeded in getting airborne. As they had come in, so they left, in a suicidal dash at rooftop level, through a hail of exploding anti-aircraft shells.

Von Greim and Hanna were strapped in behind the pilot, who threw the aircraft into a sequence of violent manoeuvres to avoid obvious concentrations of flak. Hanna was reading a sheet of paper by the dim light of a pocket torch, and when she finished, with a scornful smile she screwed the piece of paper into a ball and threw it out into the night.

'What was that?' von Greim asked in some surprise.

'Eva Braun's letter.'

'Then what the devil did you throw it away for?'

'For the Fuehrer,' Hanna said.

'But Eva Braun is the Fuehrer's mistress!'

'Exactly.'

Von Greim stared at her, astonished. She had a savage little smile on her face, and seeing that von Greim failed utterly to understand, she explained, 'It was such a vulgar little letter. You can't imagine how cheap and theatrical that woman's mind is. Ugh! And had that letter been saved for posterity, it could only have harmed the memory of the man capable of loving such a woman . . .'

Down below in a Berlin now almost completely taken over by the Russians, a pile of Iron Crosses lay scattered on the ground. Beside them was the body of the pretty young auxiliary of the Volkssturm. She was dead. Running past her, illuminated by the light of an exploding rocket, a young Russian soldier carried an enormous red flag across a street raked by machine gun bullets. It was only a matter of a few hours before it would all be at an end.

Just as dawn broke, a small man in a grey and very worn civilian suit stumbled along one of the approaches to the Bunker. Ahead of him ran a squad of German machine gunners firing into the dark. The man, who was being half dragged along by two hefty SS guards, was City Councillor Walter Wagner, Qualified Official of the Reich. He was in poor physical shape and was very, very frightened. He had no idea why he had been sent for in such a desperate hurry. But he suspected the worst.

It was the penultimate day of the ten, 29 April 1945. Wagner was ushered into Dr Goebbels' room in the Bunker, accompanied by the two guards. He was panting from his exertions and his apprehension increased when he saw the grim frown Goebbels gave him after a critical inspection of his creased and dusty suit.

'Heil Hitler!' Councillor Wagner said nervously, but Goebbels' continued to stalk round him, staring at him with cold disapproval. 'What has happened, Herr Minister? What do you wish me to do?'

'Herr Wagner!' Goebbels said sternly, 'you come here in these clothes?'

Now Wagner became even more frightened. He started stammering. 'But I . . . I haven't got a uniform. I can't fight. I tried to volunteer. Really I did. But as you know, Herr Minister, I've suffered for years from angina pectoris. They wouldn't take me.'

'Yes, yes,' Goebbels said irritably, 'I know all that. That's not the problem. No, look here, don't you have a dark suit?' Wagner was almost speechless with surprise and total incomprehension. Why had he been brought so dangerously to the Bunker at the risk not only of his own life but of those of his guards, only to be asked why he hadn't put on a dark suit?

'I'm sorry, Herr Minister, actually . . . I didn't know . . . at this hour . . . well, I'd only just got into bed . . . I have to work late, you see, and . . .' His voice tailed off in confusion.

'You have come here to perform a marriage ceremony!' Dr Goebbels said authoritatively. Wagner put his hand to his heart, as though fearing an attack. 'And you can't do it dressed like that,' Goebbels said peremptorily and turned to the SS guards. 'Look everywhere! Turn the Bunker upside down! But find a dark suit for Herr Wagner and do so at once . . .'

It was only then that it dawned on the City Councillor that he had been brought to the Bunker to marry Adolf Hitler and Eva Braun.

Later on, in the meeting room of the Bunker, Hitler and Eva Braun stood in front of Herr Wagner, who was dressed in a black suit which was much too small for him. Hitler looked stiff and distant; Eva Braun was tense and emotional, biting her lower lip and looking almost on the verge of tears. Bormann and Goebbels stood beside the Fuehrer and Magda Goebbels beside Eva Braun.

She was wearing a simple black dress with two roses pinned at the neckline, and matching kid shoes, together with a large sleeveless cape with rose-red epaulettes. She was heavily made up and in addition to a pearl necklace, she had put gold clips in her hair and a diamond watch on her wrist.

Herr Wagner coughed, cleared his throat and began reading from a long, official document: 'Today, the twenty-ninth day of April 1945, I City Councillor Walter

Wagner, Qualified Official of the Capital of the Reich, have received a request for an act of marriage between Adolf Hitler, born on 20 April 1889 in Branau, domiciled in Berlin, Chancellery of the Reich, publicly known and therefore . . .'

He floundered momentarily. The implications of some of the questions which the law required him to ask the Fuehrer and his bride appalled him. He took a deep breath, '. . . and therefore not required to produce documents of identity.'

Hitler nodded curtly. Herr Wagner recoiled slightly, as if he found this almost as daunting as if the Fuehrer were going to object, '. . . and Fraulein Eva Braun, born on 2 February 1910 at Munich, Watburgstrasse, who presents as a document of identity . . .' He stopped to check that what he was going to say was accurate, '. . . a special passport issued by the Chief of the German Police Force.' Eva smiled tearfully.

'As witnesses, the Reichsminister Dr Josef Goebbels, born on 26 October 1897 at Rheydt and domiciled in Berlin, Herman Goeringstrasse 20.' Goebbels acknowledged the reference disdainfully. It was rather an unfortunately named address. '. . . and Reichsminister Martin Bormann, born on 17 June 1900 at Halberstadt and domiciled in Obersalzberg . . . the two witnesses are also publicly known and have no further need of identity documents . . .' Again Wagner came to a halt, steeling himself to put the next question to the Fuehrer. Eva looked at Hitler and shyly took his hand. But Hitler pushed it politely away and stared back at Wagner.

'My Fuehrer, and Fraulein, is it your request that I perform a wartime marriage, owing to the state of war and . . . exceptional circumstances?'

'Yes,' they spoke together.

'Is it your request that the publication of the banns be

made by word of mouth in order to prevent further delay?'

'Yes.'

Wagner coughed nervously. 'Your requests are accepted.' He glanced about wildly like a man trapped, then plunged on: 'Are you, my Fuehrer, Adolf Hitler, of pure Aryan origin?'

'Yes,' Hitler snapped.

'And you, Fraulein Eva Braun, are you of pure Aryan origin?'

'Yes.'

Wagner looked down at the next question and the colour began to rise in his face. 'Does there exist in your family, my Fuehrer, Adolf Hitler, any case of hereditary disease?'

'No.'

Herr Wagner ticked off the questions on his piece of paper. Outside and overhead the guns were booming away.

'My Fuehrer, Adolf Hitler, will you take as your wedded wife, Fraulein Eva Braun?'

'Yes.'

'And you, Fraulein Eva Braun, will you take as your wedded husband, our Fuehrer Adolf Hitler?'

'Yes,' Eva said quickly and emphatically.

'Did the witnesses hear?' Wagner asked, looking at Bormann and Goebbels. They both nodded. 'The documents now made public by word of mouth,' Wagner went on, 'have been verified and proved authentic . . . I therefore declare you man and wife to all purposes of the law.'

There were tears in Eva's eyes. Bormann, Goebbels and Wagner flung up their arms and shouted, 'Heil, my Fuehrer!' Magda Goebbels embraced the bride, weeping too. Only Hitler appeared to be unmoved. He remained curt and formal and asked Wagner, 'Is there anything else we should do, Councillor?'

F

'Only sign, my Fuehrer.'

Hitler took the document, put it on the table and stooped down to sign it. He gave the pen to Eva. She wrote her first name carefully, then began her surname 'B' . . . stopped short, smiled nervously, and began again – 'Hitler'.

THIRTY-TWO

So they were married. That evening in the dining room of the Bunker, Herr and Frau Hitler gave a small party in celebration. Eva wore a pale cream dress which was much too young for her. The celebration got off to a lame start. Goebbels struggled to open the first bottle of champagne but the cork refused to move. The little doctor's knuckles were white as he tried ineffectually to twist it out. In the end he gave up the attempt and passed the bottle to Bormann.

Hitler had his usual cup of tea and took no notice. Bormann's thick hands also failed to shift the cork and he passed the bottle irritably to General Krebs. One by one, in an embarrassed hush, the officers struggled with the cork, without success. Finally, Hoffmann rescued them all. He gripped the thing firmly, pulled hard and it came out with only the faintest hissing sound. Hoffmann filled the glasses, while Goebbels tried to rescue the situation.

'That always happens with bottles of very old vintage,' he said with a half-hearted smile. 'The quality improves but you don't get the pop.'

No one was listening. The joylessness of the scene was oppressive, and the atmosphere affected even those hardened cynics who had surrounded the Fuehrer for so long. Bormann raised his glass for a toast and Hitler matched the gesture with his cup of green tea. But words failed Bormann at this point and he could think of nothing to say.

Since the men seemed unable to cope, Magda Goebbels raised her glass. 'Everything you most desire, my Fuehrer . . . and everything *you* most desire, Eva dear . . .' Her voice was brittle with forced gaiety. Eva was touched, and not far from tears.

'Victory!' she cried. They all drank. Once more they were in the grip of an embarrased silence.

Finally Hitler drained his cup of tea and remarked, 'This is still the champagne we brought back from Paris, isn't it, Goebbels?'

'Yes, my Fuehrer . . .'

'When I was a witness at your wedding, Goebbels there was no champagne of this quality,' Hitler said, looking at his teacup with a smile. 'Of course, that was before we conquered the French . . .' he paused and thought of Paris. 'In Paris there is a magnificent opera house, Eva,' he said. 'It is the only good thing the French have achieved in the realm of art . . . all the rest is degenerate . . . especially in painting.' He broke off, lost in thought again. No one spoke. They had all heard it all so many times before.

'The English have no art at all,' Hitler went on in the end. 'In no country in the world do they perform Shakespeare as badly as in England. In the whole of Great Britain, there is only one opera house and even that one doesn't bear comparison with the smallest among our hundred German opera houses.' He shook his head sadly; the artist in him appalled by these deficiencies. 'And yet they are so proud of their democracy! But what have democracies ever accomplished of historical value? How many great buildings, how many monuments, how many domes have they created? Can you name me a single great army which was given birth to in a democracy? Can you tell me of any democracy which ever conquered a continent?'

'None, my Fuehrer,' said Bormann. 'Certainly none.'

'In the democracies every mediocre person strives to have his share of power . . . the only result is chaos and weakness of the nation . . . the people don't want democracy . . . the people want all power concentrated in the hands of a strong man, who will be able to maintain law and order . . .'

'How right you are, my Fuehrer,' Goebbels was the only one who managed to look as if he'd never heard the monotonous monologue before.

'The best proof of this is the fact that National Socialism rode to power on the people's vote. I didn't make a revolution . . . I beat my opponents at the polls . . . it was the great masses who chose me!'

He laughed sardonically. 'And yet I'm being accused of abolishing elections in Germany! But what is the use of elections when the people have already clearly expressed their will? They wanted me to make decisions for them, they entrusted their country and their lives to me. And once the people have chosen, what good is it to make them choose over and over again every year?' He had worked himself up to a shout. 'The people *have* chosen! The only one to benefit from the mire of a democratic government is that filthy clique of Jews from whom, by choice of destiny, I have tried to free the world.'

Hoffmann had been listening to this tirade in stupefaction. Bormann who was next to him and who had been watching him out of the corner of his eye, leaned over and murmured, 'What a great experience it must be for you to hear such profound thoughts for the first time . . . and at your age!' Hoffmann stared back at him, speechless. Bormann was too blind to realise that Hoffmann was tongue-tied by incredulity, not adulation.

Hitler ranted on. 'Can I ever forget how before I came

to power all the industrialists of so-called democratic Germany came to me and begged me to take the reins firmly in my hands to protect their factories and their privileges? I listened to their cries for help. I protected them. I had their war factories going full blast . . . And today – what happens? Who has seen one of these gentlemen, like Herr Thyssen, Herr Krupp, Herr Roechling, Herr Otto Wolff and all the high and mighty others? Where are they now?'

'They are all traitors, my Fuehrer,' cried Bormann. 'We shall settle accounts with them after the victory.'

Hitler stopped speaking. He handed his cup to Eva, who filled it again. He began to sip it slowly. A look of contentment crossed his face. Blondi, sat beside him and he patted the dog reflectively. 'That is why I love dogs more than humans. They are more faithful and often more intelligent. They are brave and more beautiful.' He gazed fondly at the dog. 'What a pity that Blondi must die because of all those treacherous humans.'

A stunned silence followed this bald observation. Eva looked at her husband, and tried to hide the prickling fear which had begun to creep through her. To her surprise, Hitler smiled at her affectionately. 'Eva, please . . . the gifts for our guests.'

'Yes, Adolf dear . . .'

THIRTY-THREE

Eva went to a cupboard and lifted out a big rectangular box which she carried across to Hitler. The Fuehrer stood up and so did everyone else. He took the box and together they distributed the 'going away presents'. There was one for everyone, a photograph of the Fuehrer in a silver frame and a small cardboard box. 'A little personal souvenir of this day,' Hitler explained as she started to hand them out.

There were polite murmurs of appreciation. Then Hitler added, pointing to the little boxes, 'Each box contains two cyanide capsules. They are the same kind as my wife and I will use.' Bormann took his presents and thanked the Fuehrer vigorously. Burgdorf was almost in tears. Voss moved not a muscle of his face, but Hoffmann accepted his gift with ill-concealed revulsion.

When the couple reached Fraulein Junge and Frau Christian, Eva said impulsively, 'Ladies, if you will let me, I want you to have my two silver fox furs.'

They were both too moved to answer. Hitler turned away frowning and offered his gifts to the Goebbels. 'This isn't the present I was hoping to give you at the end of the war, Magda my dear,' Hitler said. She pressed a handkerchief to her mouth and was unable to look up. Goebbels, however said, 'You haven't got six more of those boxes, my Fuehrer? For my children ...'

'Have we any more, Eva?' Hitler asked, with as much emotion as if he were enquiring of an assistant about a line of jam.

'I'm afraid not, Adolf dear.'

Hitler turned with an urbane smile to Dr Stumpfegger, 'Herr Doktor, what would you suggest?'

'Offhand, I'd say three hundred cc's of morphine intravenously.'

'That's the answer, then.'

'Thank you, my Fuehrer ...'

The ceremony was over and Hitler murmured to Fraulein Junge, 'Fraulein, would you be kind enough to come with me to my study? I know it is very late but there is something I absolutely must dictate now.'

'At once, my Fuehrer.'

He turned to Eva, and said quietly, 'Eva, would you mind entertaining the guests with one of your pretty little songs?'

He left the room, followed by Fraulein Junge. The atmosphere remained tense and oppressive. One or two people looked inside the boxes. Only Eva tried to rise to the occasion. 'Come on, Bormann,' she ordered. 'Open up another bottle of champagne. This is a feast day. Now, on the Fuehrer's orders I'm going to sing you all a song . . .' Bormann began struggling clumsily with the next bottle, while Eva, with a pathetic attempt at brightness, began to hum the opening bars of one of her favourite songs of the 'twenties. Then with a slight quaver in the voice which she gradually overcame, she began to sing the words, 'Tea for two . . . and two for tea, And me for you . . . and you for me . . .'

A few people were smirking at the amateurish performance, but most of them were glad of any effort that might lift the leaden atmosphere. Bormann laced his champagne with a strong dose of brandy and passed the bottle round to the others. Everyone relaxed. They began to move about and chat and laugh while Eva continued to sing and dance alone in the centre of the room.

Hoffmann walked over to Krebs who, like Bormann, had helped himself liberally to the brandy. 'General Krebs, what do you think the Fuehrer is doing in his study?'

The general drained his glass with a dramatic gesture. 'Perhaps we have been witnesses to his farewell, Captain . . . perhaps history has summoned us to witness his last farewell . . .' He stopped and smiled at Eva who had begun another of her favourite songs, from a Fred Astaire talky.

Bormann was no longer there. He had slipped away, unseen by the others, and gone to the darkened meeting room. He walked gingerly towards the Fuehrer's chair and leaning over the disordered map table, switched on

135

a desk light. An unexpected noise startled him and he jumped back, his eyes on the door. But no one came in. Everything was quiet again and with a look of savage satisfaction on his face, he lowered himself slowly into the Fuehrer's chair.

THIRTY-FOUR

The news of the Fuehrer's wedding swept round the Bunker like a fire. In the main corridors and mess halls there was a rising hubbub of conviviality. The last vestiges of military formality crumbled and officers – some with their collars undone – mingled with non-commissioned officers and civilians. Dozens of extra bottles were brought out and handed around.

The 'secure' door to the outer quarters (and ultimately to the staircase and the outer world) was guarded only intermittently, and an SS officer came in, bespattered with rain and mud, straight into an astonishing scene. He saw a friend in the crowd – a Wehrmacht officer – and pushed a way through to him.

'What's going on here?'

'Our Fuehrer has just got married.'

'*What*?'

'It's true.'

'Unbelievable!' Then, as an afterthought, 'Who to?'

'Fraulein Braun – so they say.'

'Fraulein Braun. Who *is* Fraulein Braun?'

A burst of applause and cheering distracted them both. The mood of the crowd in the Bunker was becoming increasingly riotous, not so much from joy at the Fuehrer's marriage as from the excuse to get drunk and open up the stores. Bottles of wine and schnapps were dragged in by the case. Foods of all kinds were being carried in and were quickly grabbed and eaten. Tins of caviare, meats, jars of fruit – all the forbidden luxuries of the last years of the war were devoured with frenetic greed. An SS guard seized one of the nurses and half playfully bent her back to kiss her. They both fell to the floor and began writhing about while the people standing nearby laughed and cheered.

Outside the bunker entrance where the Russians shells were thundering down incessantly, several SS and a few Wehrmacht soldiers stood around with bottles of alcohol in their hands. They had dragged a few girls off the Berlin streets – half starved and in tattered clothes. One of them was voraciously eating a piece of cake while an SS man kissed her neck and shoulders and then began nuzzling her breasts. She paid no attention but simply continued to gorge herself on the cake. A couple of soldiers came up the stairs carrying more food with them and two or three of the bolder girls went down in search of the source. All the time the singing, drinking, gorging and overt sexuality increased. It had already passed the pitch of the wildest New Year's Eve party any of them had ever known.

In the Fuehrer's dining room, Eva's own party was in full swing. Eva, flushed from her exertions and the champagne, was doing one of her favourite turns – a take-off of Al Jolson. Empty champagne bottles littered the room.

Girls from the streets came down the staircase in droves, some out of curiosity, others because they were dragged down by the SS guards. There was laughter, screaming, singing and shouting. One girl, pulled handfuls of bread off a long loaf and stuffed them into her mouth while two SS men tore off her clothes. She took no notice at all. Nearby a pile of military greatcoats provided a makeshift bed for a soldier and a girl to make love. Gas mask containers and other rubbish lay about the corridors. One couple were making love on a stretcher on the corridor floor; another pair had broken into the surgery and lay together on the operating table.

In the Emergency Telephone Room, the big telephone switchboard was dark and disused, the plugs hanging idly at the end of their cables. Half a dozen soldiers and girls lay about half-dressed or naked, drinking and making love.

In the Dental Surgery the Countess was sitting astride a young officer on the dental chair.

'Promise?' she said, 'When you're on guard?' He nodded and she kissed him. 'Promise to let me into his room?' He nodded and pulled her face towards him. 'Word of honour? As a soldier? You'll let me touch him?' He promised. The Countess moaned a low, harsh animal sound. 'My Fuehrer! I want to touch you! Your eyes!' She shuddered and cried out, her body taut and upright, her head bent back and her mouth open ...

Hitler sat in his study, his steel framed spectacles on his nose, reading through some pages of typing. On the other side of the table stood Bormann and Goebbels. Now and then, the sounds of the 'revelry' outside broke into the quiet of the study. Bormann leaned over and said softly to Goebbels, 'We must get those swine to stop . . .'

Hitler looked up over the top of his papers. 'Leave them alone, Bormann . . . as long as they're not smoking . . .'

He returned to his reading and then, without getting up, handed over the sheets to the other two. Removing his glasses he said solemnly: 'Gentlemen, I have just dictated my final political testament. I have been compelled to make it upon the supposition that General Wenck's army will not arrive.'

He caught a flicker of greed in Bormann's eyes and

immediately said, 'I know what you're thinking, Bormann. But you are quite perfect in your present position. Instead, I have appointed Doenitz as my successor . . . you, my dear Goebbels, are to be the Reichschancellor . . .' He saw that they would both protest and shut them up with his usual authority. 'No! No! I don't want you to say anything. It is necessary for the continuity of the Party and the government.'

THIRTY-FIVE

Hitler had never been sparing with words, and in his last political testament he remained true to form, never using one word where three or four would do the job as well.

'More than thirty years have passed,' it began, 'since I made my modest contribution as a volunteer in the First World War which the Reich was then forced to fight. In these three decades, love and loyalty to my people alone have guided me in all my thoughts, my actions and life. They gave me power to make the most difficult decisions which have ever confronted mortal man . . .

'It is untrue that I or anyone else in Germany wanted war in 1939. It was wanted and provoked exclusively by those international statesmen who were either of Jewish origin or worked for Jewish interests. I have made too many offers for the limitation and control of armaments, which posterity will not for all time be able to disregard, for the responsibility for the outbreak of this war to be placed on me. Centuries will go by but from the ruins of our towns and monuments, the hatred of those ultimately responsible will always grow anew. They are the ones we have to thank for all this: international Jewry and its supporters . . .'

In a corner of the surgery, Dr Stumpfegger and two ambulance men were forcing open the mouth of Hitler's dog, and pushing a phial of cyanide down her throat. Nearby an SS guard put his pistol against each of her puppies in turn and shot them.

Goebbels and Bormann read on. 'My reasonable proposition for the solution of a German-Polish problem was rejected only because the mob who were in power in England insisted on war, partly for commercial reasons, partly because they were influenced by the propaganda organised by international Jewry. After six years of a war which, in spite of its reverses, will one day go down in history as the most glorious and heroic manifestation of a nation's struggle for existence, I cannot forsake the city which is the capital of this state . . .'

In the Goebbels' apartment, Magda Goebbels' six children were all happily playing a war game, tearing their room in the Bunker inside out.

'But I shall not fall into the hands of an enemy who needs a new spectacle exhibited by the Jews to divert the hysterical masses . . . I have decided to choose death voluntarily at the moment when I consider my position as Fuehrer and Chancellor itself can no longer be maintained.'

In the corridors of the Bunker, SS guards, sated with gastronomic and sexual excess, lay asleep on benches and on the floor.

'I die with a joyful heart in my knowledge of the immeasurable deeds and achievements of our peasants and workers, and of a contribution, unequalled in history, of our youth who bears my name. I exhort the commanders of the three branches of our glorious armed forces to strengthen with every possible means the spirit of resistance of our soldiers in the National Socialist belief, with special emphasis that I myself, the founder and creator

140

of the movement, choose death rather than a cowardly capitulation.'

Eva Hitler was searching through her wardrobe for a new and very beautiful, embroidered nightdress.

'Above all I order the government and the people to maintain the racial laws in all their severity and to pledge themselves to mercilessly resist that poisoner of all nations, international Jewry. My possessions, in so far as they are worth anything, belong to the Party, or, if this no longer exists, to the State. If the State, too is destroyed, there is no need for any further instructions on my part.'

The Countess was carefully making up her face, using the mirror in one of the Bunker lavatories.

'The paintings in the collections bought by me during the course of the years were never assembled for private purposes, but solely for the establishment of a picture gallery in my home town of Linz on the Danube. As executor, I appoint Martin Bormann, who is given full legal authority to hand over to my relatives anything which is a personal memento or is necessary to maintain a lower middle class standard of living . . .'

Fraulein Manzialy stood in the kitchen, wiping her hands on her apron, and assembling the ingredients for the next meal.

'Although during the years of struggle I believed that I could not undertake the responsibility of marriage, now before the end of my life, I have decided to take as my wife the woman who, after many years of true friendship, came to this city, already besieged, of her own free will, in order to share my fate. She will go to her death with me at her own wish, as my wife. This will compensate us for what we both lost through my work in the service of my people.

'My wife and I choose to die in order to escape the shame of defeat or capitulation. It is our wish that our bodies shall be burnt immediately in the place where I

141

have performed the greater part of my daily life during the course of my twelve years' service to my people . . .'

Late that night, Bormann sat in his room, deep in thought; then he picked up a pen, and on the pad in front of him began slowly and laboriously to write down a list. It began, 'Bormann, President, Fuehrer and Chancellor of the Reich. Goebbels, Minister for Foreign Affairs . . .'

Outside, Hitler roamed the last few hundred square feet of his empire. He was stooped and shuffling so slowly and so quietly that the sleeping SS did not stir. He was defeated, destroyed in every fibre of his body; but his eyes still retained their hypnotic power, the cold light of hatred that had always lurked in them. He limped on through his miserable palace of reinforced concrete, shattered continually by the impact of bursting shells. Closed into himself, in his egocentric silence, he was like a ghost which haunted the still terrifying shadow of an epoch that was on the way out.

THIRTY-SIX

It was 30 April 1945. Hoffmann stood in the Switchboard Room of the Bunker, haggard, hollow-eyed and unshaven. There was still one working telephone and on the wall was a large map of Berlin, with the Bunker in the middle, on which he was trying to draw the front line as it closed even more tightly around the central point.

Krebs came in behind him. 'Anything new?'

'They have passed the Belle Alliance Platz . . . they're heading this way.'

'From which command did you get the news?'

'Command?' Hoffmann said bitterly, 'No command at all. All radio contacts are now cut off. I'm receiving information from the people of Berlin. I pick numbers out of the telephone book.' He started to dial another number.

'That's not a reliable method,' Krebs said indignantly, but Hoffmann gestured at him not to talk. He had picked the number of the town house of one of Germany's oldest aristocratic families, the von Zitzewitzes. The number rang for a long time and was finally answered. The voice was that of an elderly woman, but it was firm and authoritative.

'Hello . . . what? . . . This *is* Frau Zitzewitz . . .' Hoffmann held the phone a little away so that Krebs could hear.

'Yes, of course I've seen the Russians . . . they were here about half an hour ago . . . they had a dozen tanks . . . no, there was no street fighting here . . . but who is this speaking, please?'

Hoffmann explained, slowly and clearly. There was a long pause as the old lady assimilated the extraordinary information. Then she burst out, 'You mean it seriously? You are still *there*? Well, you can tell the Fuehrer that he is a great liar and that I've thrown his portrait away . . . he ought never to have done a thing like that, letting the Russians right into our city – and our homes . . . after all the things he said.'

The phone went dead and Hoffmann put down his receiver too. He and Krebs looked at each other with raised eyebrows and then on impulse Hoffmann dialled another number. It was answered by a child's voice. 'Hello,' Hoffmann said in a more gentle tone, 'Isn't there anyone older than you at home? Your mother, perhaps? . . . you're alone? . . . Have you seen the Russians? . . . yes, I understand . . . you're all by yourself . . . no, don't cry . . . someone will come . . . very soon.'

Hoffmann hung up quickly. Krebs came as close to

looking upset as was possible in a Wehrmacht General. 'That was a child?'

'Yes, but a very young one. He didn't even know what Russians are, lucky boy.'

He dialled again. 'Hallo . . .' The bitter surprise on his face became an ironic smile. He held the receiver out to Krebs. 'Listen, General . . .' Krebs took the instrument and listened. There was an outburst of Russian, and the noise of shouting and firing in the background. Krebs handed the receiver back to Hoffmann who put it down. 'That was the house of an old school friend of mine,' Hoffmann explained in a sombre voice, 'half a mile from here . . . even less than that . . .'

Outside Frau Hitler's room, a maid knocked quietly on the door, entered the room cautiously, went to the bed and bent over Eva. She spoke softly, 'Fraulein Braun . . .'

Eva was already awake, and opened her eyes, and stretched luxuriously. 'You may safely call me Frau Hitler now,' she yawned.

The maid was embarrassed. 'I'm sorry, Frau Hitler.'

Eva smiled at her. She got out of bed in her beautiful, immaculate nightdress and went to the mirror. 'What time is it? Is the Fuehrer awake?'

'I don't know, Frau Hitler.'

'Is it a nice day outside?' The girl nodded. 'I knew it would be. You know, Liesl, that I can always feel the weather?' The girl nodded again. 'And do you know what I'm going to do this morning? I am going to have breakfast with my husband . . .'

The girl smiled. 'You mean you're going to sacrifice your first cigarette?'

Eva sighed. 'Those are the burdens of married life, Liesl. But it's well worth it . . . you go and get breakfast ready. I'll call you.'

The Fuehrer was lying on his bed completely dressed. He was fast asleep but had not removed even his cap or shoes. Eva came into the room, dressed in a beautifully made, diaphanous peignoir. The room was lit only by a single, dim table lamp and it was only when she had tip-toed to the bed, hoping to surprise him, that she realised he was asleep. She stood looking at him tenderly for a while, and shook her head, then she bent down to kiss him. As she straightened up, she bumped into the lamp which crashed to the floor and went out. In the darkness Hitler's frightened voice cried out, 'Who is it? What's happening?'

Eva stumbled over to the door and put on the central light. Hitler sat up on the bed, pale-faced, panic-stricken.

'I'm sorry if I woke you up, dear.'

'What is it, then? A telegram?'

'You've been awake all night? Why didn't you get undressed?'

Hitler spoke to her as if she were a member of his General Staff, 'In case of emergency, nobody must find the Fuehrer in his pyjamas . . . what did you want then, Eva? I thought . . . I was dreaming of a telegram . . .'

'A *telegram*? From whom, dearest?'

'That damned cigar smoker, Churchill – or Stalin.'

Eva was confused. It wasn't what she expected at all. 'I don't know . . . I don't think so . . .'

Hitler got off the bed and went to his desk. 'Strange . . . very strange . . . then I must have been dreaming. Yet the conflicts between them must be growing . . . they need me . . . I feel it with my intuition. They'll telephone . . . sooner than you might think. Today probably. In a few hours.'

THIRTY-SEVEN

The last meeting of the War Council began. There was only one map left on the table, a map of Berlin. Around it stood Generals Krebs and Burgdorf, Admiral Voss and Captain Hoffmann – all that was left of the once proud concourse of the German High Command. Hitler still sat in silence in his huge black chair, but the others looked hollow-cheeked, with tired, reddened eyes. No one had shaved.

Bormann and Goebbels were there too. They were the only political or Party connections left in contact with the Fuehrer. They listened expressionlessly as Krebs delineated the disastrous situation.

'There is a growing danger of our forces in Berlin itself being cut in two. The critical point is the western zone of the Tiergarten. The Wilmersdorf district is almost completely surrounded. There is now only a frail link with the area of the Havel Bridge, which is defended and held by the Hitler Youth.'

At that moment a violent explosion shook the bunker. Heavy blocks of cement crashed from the ceiling and the room filled with dust. Hitler interrupted Krebs' report and lay a shaking hand on Hoffmann's arm. Anchoring himself by the arm of the chair with his other hand, he turned slowly towards him, his ashen face twitching with fear. 'What calibre are they using? Do you think they can destroy the Bunker? You've been at the front, Captain Hoffmann. You should know, shouldn't you?'

Hoffmann had difficulty in keeping the contempt he felt from showing. He replied in a matter-of-fact, almost off-hand way. 'Well, it's certainly at least a 17.5 calibre.

In my opinion the calibre and the force of the impact are not sufficient to destroy the Bunker.' He pursed his lips drily, as if such questions were purely academic. Hitler seemed reassured and motioned to Krebs to go on.

'The Russians are advancing down the Wilhelmstrasse. At this point they can't be more than half a mile away. They are also advancing down the Potsdamerstrasse, whilst our troops are still offering staunch resistance between the Kanstrasse and the Bismarckstrasse.' This seemed to exhaust the disastrous military news. Bormann looked up.

'Yes, Bormann?'

'My Fuehrer, we have monitored a radio broadcast from a neutral source. It reports – it reports tragically that this morning the Duce of Fascism . . . Benito Mussolini . . . has been killed by the Italian Communists of Badoglio. His body and that of his – friend, Signorina Pettacci, were . . . hung up in the main square in Milan.'

No one moved. Hitler looked down. He seemed changed to stone. His left arm began shaking; he bit his upper lip and seemed on the point of tears.

'Say nothing of this to Frau Eva, Bormann . . . Mussolini was a loyal friend . . . weak . . . a victim of his monarchy . . . of that corkscrew king!' He paused in thought. 'Ah! Mussolini, he should have swept it all away, long before . . . they have betrayed him . . . just as they betrayed me. It is the destiny of all superior men to be betrayed . . . from Christ on . . .'

He tried to talk back into himself the nervous energy he needed and which he could no longer find. 'He had great vices, poor Mussolini . . . but great virtues as well. He was the first to understand my genius – the first foreign head of state who shook hands with me and remained loyal to me to the end.' His train of thought took him off at a tangent. 'In his way he, too, was an artist . . . he played the violin, you know . . .' The voice tailed off again. 'They must have tortured and outraged their bodies,' he went on, 'Even after death we must not fall into the hands of our enemies . . .'

Again he paused. Then, regaining a little of his old force, he went on more sharply, 'It is essential that my testament be put in safe keeping. It is too important for the generation to come. Every risk – every negative possibility must be forestalled . . . I shall personally select the four most loyal officers in the Bunker . . . yes – four officers . . . and they will go north, south, east and west. At least one of them will get through.'

THIRTY-EIGHT

A little later that day four officers, Hoffmann among them, stood to attention in front of the Fuehrer in the study. Hoffmann's eyes were dulled, remote, far away, and when Hitler spoke, they no longer responded with any interest at all.

Slowly, solemnly, Hitler gave to each of them a sealed red folder. He handed the last folder to Hoffmann. '. . . and this goes to Feldmarschall Schoerner. Gentlemen, bear it well in mind; these few typed pages are sacred. It would be an irreparable catastrophe if they came to be lost. Naturally you will answer for them with your lives.' He dismissed them with a nod.

Hoffmann and the others gave the Nazi salute. 'Heil, my Fuehrer!'

Hitler left the room, followed by Bormann and Goebbels. Krebs heaved a long sigh and said with heavy theatricality: 'Gentlemen, I am afraid that what we have just witnessed was – a farewell.'

So Hoffmann left the Bunker at the eleventh hour through the smoke of incendiaries and amid the thunder of shell and bomb explosions. He had not gone very far when he came upon a girl of fifteen or sixteen trying to tear off the planks from a wooden bench. She lacked the strength to do so and was going about it in the wrong way, so that her hands bled. But she was determined not to give up.

She cursed through her teeth, trying to encourage herself, and then Hoffmann's shadow fell across her and she whipped round guiltily and aggressively. For a moment or so they studied each other. Then Hoffmann asked, 'What are you doing that for? You known it's forbidden.'

'So what? It's all kaput. Everything's kaput. What are *you* going to do? Shoot me?' Hoffmann put down his bag. Although his uniform was far from clean, it looked immaculate compared with the tatters the girl wore. They looked at each other for a moment or so, then Hoffmann produced a packet of biscuits from his pocket and offered them to the girl, who grabbed them before he could have second thoughts and started cramming them into her mouth.

'Where do you live?'

'Somewhere in the rubble over there.'

'Got anybody – any family?'

'How would I know? I *had* a father and a brother. God knows where they are. Where have *you* been in the last few days?' Hoffmann looked at her without answering. The air crackled with rifle fire. He still carried the Fuehrer's testament in his hand. 'Do you want to die?' the girl asked brutally.

Hoffmann managed a smile. 'Not particularly – no.'

'Then why don't you take that fucking uniform off?' She understood dimly that he must be somebody special in spite of his youth. As he still said nothing, she went on with the frankness of the gutter, 'Heroes are all shits, didn't you know?' Hoffmann nodded, but it was an effort.

In some way this seemed to move her. A shell landed closer than before, but neither of them flinched or moved.

'You don't have a suit belonging to your brother, do you? A civilian suit?'

'It'd be too big for you,' she said with a flash of contempt, and then with a look at the planks, 'but what the hell do you care? You've obviously been eating lately. You've got a bit of muscle, I can see.'

She pointed at the wood. 'Bring that along. We shall need it if we're going to survive the next few days.' She began to move away. Hoffmann looked after her, then he tore the Fuehrer's last testament into pieces and scattered them in the wind. He went to the bench and stripped it of its wood.

THIRTY-NINE

In the Bunker, in the anteroom to Hitler's study, only Bormann, Goebbels, Krebs and Voss were left. They paced up and down in a state of acute nervous tension, scarcely ever taking their eyes off the closed door of the Fuehrer's study. Occasionally one or another of them sat down for a moment or so but the restlessness was contagious. All ears were cocked to catch the slightest unnatural noise.

Suddenly Goebbels leaped to his feet and limped determinedly across to the door. 'I'm going in to see . . . I can't help it . . . he's been shut in there for two hours.'

'With his wife, Dr Goebbels,' Bormann observed, cautious even unto death. Goebbels stopped and looked from him to Krebs and Voss. No one knew what to do.

'What if he *is* dead?' Goebbels asked. No one answered. Eventually Goebbels turned away from the door.

'Shall we make a compromise, Dr Goebbels?' Bormann said. 'It is two o'clock exactly . . . if he has given no sign of life by three, we shall all enter his room together.' Goebbels did not reply. He sat down again in silence.

Then suddenly, without warning, the study door opened and Hitler appeared in the doorway. 'I am hungry, gentlemen. Bring me my lunch. Only for me. My wife is not hungry . . .' The four of them looked at him in amazement, as if he were risen from the dead. 'In the meantime, I have had an idea, General Krebs. Since the Russians can walk in *under* our defences through the tunnels of the Underground and attack us from the rear, you should immediately give orders to open all the locks on the Spree to flood the Underground.'

Krebs was horrified. 'But, my Fuehrer, the tunnels of the Underground are now our field hospitals. There are thousands of wounded soldiers down there. Thousands of women and children . . . old people. They would all be drowned.'

'At a time like this, General Krebs, the supreme thought of every German is the salvation of the Reich and National Socialism. Not human lives.'

His voice was hard, adamant. 'Have them open all the Spree locks immediately.'

'But . . . but, my Fuehrer . . .'

'Do it.'

So the last horror was imposed on the Berliners by the Fuehrer himself. In the Underground tunnels, which already resembled battlefields, where the wounded lay everywhere untended and waiting for death, where the stench of excrement made the air all but unbreathable, the river water came bursting along the railway lines, flooding over benches and stretchers, over children, women, old people and the wounded, sweeping them all away in a crescendo of screaming despair.

Panic and terror were rife as they all tried at once to run before the flood, as they stumbled and fell, as children were trampled underfoot and thousands upon thousands were lost in the fury of the current storming through the open locks of the Spree.

Meanwhile, Hitler was served with a substantial lunch. Frau Christian and Fraulein Junge sat at the table with him and Fraulein Manzialy hovered nearby. Hitler looked at them only fleetingly. He put out a hand to stop Fraulein Manzialy from removing the plate with the omelette from the table. He took a second helping and went on eating in silence.

As he gave his mouth a final wipe with his napkin, the door opened and Krebs appeared, followed in by Bormann and Goebbels. Hitler looked at them with raised eyebrows, and the three women hurried out of the room.

'My Fuehrer,' Krebs said, 'the tunnels of the Underground have been flooded. The locks on the Spree have been blown up.'

'Good, General Krebs,' Hitler said calmly.

After a moment's hesitation, Krebs continued: 'Despite this measure, my Fuehrer, Russian guns have appeared in the very neighbourhood of this Bunker . . . making all resistance practically useless.'

It was the coup de grace. Hitler remained quite still for a moment or so and then said, as if every word were steeped in acid, 'For years I have been stomaching the bad news you keep bringing me, gentlemen of the General Staff . . . now I've had enough! I'm sick to death of it!'

Abruptly, he got up and left the room.

FORTY

The die was cast. Together with Eva he said goodbye to his court. The farewell occurred in the Fuehrer's study and everyone who was left was called in. Hitler's face was stony. Eva had put on a dark dress and was red-eyed from weeping. Her nerve had broken now, in company with the other women, she was openly and unashamedly crying.

Magda Goebbels stood with her six children beside Bormann, Krebs and the others, and everyone was caught up in the overwhelming poignancy of the ceremony – the last the Fuehrer would ever conduct. Even then – at the very end of it all – Hitler's strong sense of occasion did not desert him. He lived up to the image of the strange, mystic invincible Fuehrer which he had created. He did not speak.

Shaking hands with the men, nodding briefly in answer to the last salutes they would ever give him, he stopped for a moment in front of each of the women, and looked them in the eyes. That was all. It was the end.

But just as the ceremony was about to finish, the Countess suddenly appeared. She was extravagantly dressed in a long, black dress which accentuated the whiteness of her neck, her distracted face and even the pale glow of her magnificent pearls. To everyone's astonishment, she ran towards the Fuehrer, her eyes round, wild and desperate. Then, going down on one knee before him, she snatched his hand, joined it to Eva's and kissed them both, crying out tragically, 'My Fuehrer, my Fuehrer! In the name of God, what is to become of National Socialism?' It was not quite what the Fuehrer had expected, and he looked at her with some confusion. 'Do you think, my Fuehrer,' she raved on, 'that National Socialism will survive us?'

Hitler's expression changed. Tragedy and cruelty vied with each other for possession of his face and his voice became oracular. 'No, Countess, no. The German people have failed the test of history. National Socialism will die with me. Nobody will talk about Germany again for centuries. This land will be left a heap of ruins where only stray dogs roam . . .' So saying, he freed himself from her, and, followed by Eva, walked out of the room.

They walked into the Fuehrer's bedroom and Eva seated herself miserably on a small sofa, watching with apprehension as Hitler began slowly pacing the room. Finally he tok two phials of poison from one drawer and a pistol from another. She eyed him tearfully.

'You . . . you don't think we could put it off? A little while longer . . . ?'

Hitler shook his head. 'I had hoped to die on the fifth of May like Napoleon. But somebody betrayed me once again. The Russians are less than three hundred yards away. Not even flooding the underground has held them up.' He stopped beside her. She took his hand and gently stroked it.

'And you are quite sure there is no hope – neither for you nor for Germany?'

He looked into the distance, a look of great sadness in his cold blue eyes.

'There has been no hope for two years. Since the third of February 1943 when Paulus betrayed me at Stalingrad.'

Eva froze in total surprise. An expression of anguish crossed her face. Mechanically she took the cyanide capsule which Hitler held out to her and murmured like a bewildered child, 'You knew *then*? In 1943?'

Hitler was unaware of the effect his words were having

on her. He went on in a matter of fact way, 'After Stalin-grad, I realised that the Germans were too weak to hold out. Since then, I have been alone with my iron will. I had the duty to go on.'

'But *why*? When you knew so many would have to give up their lives?' She put her head in her hands and gave herself to an uncontrollable bout of tears. Hitler sat down beside her.

'It was my duty to continue the struggle. If the gods give their love only to those who demand the impossible, then our Lord gives his blessing to him who perseveres amidst the impossible . . .' He tried to caress her but she was huddled into herself with misery.

'Nature is cruel. So I, too, must be cruel. For history, the lives of millions of mediocre and simple people are of no account. They have never been and never will be.' Eva choked through her tears, 'But I am a simple, mediocre woman.'

He lifted his head arrogantly. 'You were, until I chose you . . . and from that moment, you were no longer a simple woman.'

'But for the others . . . for what happened to them, I can't understand you.'

'Eva!'

'Forgive me . . . I am not able to understand you any more . . . forgive me . . .'

He got up from the sofa. His expression began to change. His face twisted as he tried to control his rage.

'If you don't understand, then you have failed me. Both as a wife and as a German. That, as an ordinary woman whom nature has not equipped to understand the depth of purpose in a man – that such a person does not understand me I could forgive! But *you* . . .!' Eva watched him with tears pouring down her cheeks. 'You, Eva, whom destiny – through me – has singled out for a greater purpose and at the ultimate moment betrays!'

He turned away. She took the glass phial and put it into her mouth. Her eyes never left him.

'Eva, you too have failed me!' There was a crunch of glass as she bit through the phial. But he did not hear it.

'You, Eva – even you, the one woman among the thousands of women I have honoured – the one I made my own, made my wife, placed higher in the rank of womanhood even than my own mother – you, too, along with so many others I trusted, you too have . . .' He turned to glance at her and his words died away.

Eva's eyes and mouth were open, her lips slightly swollen from the cyanide. She was dead.

Hitler stared at her. His last audience had gone. He was silent – and completely still.

Outside the Fuehrer's study, Krebs, Bormann and Goebbels were waiting. They too were silent and still. Then came the sound of a muffled gun shot. All three leaped to their feet, raced for the door and burst into the room.

Eva lay on the sofa where she had collapsed. There was no blood. Hitler lay beside her, a gun hanging from his lifeless hand, his head shattered by a bullet.

After a moment, Bormann went across to them cautiously, like a cat. He bent over Hitler's body and put his ear to the heart. Then, taking a piece of mirror from his pocket, he placed it in front of their lips, first one and then the other. Then he straightened up and looked at Goebbels, shaking his head.

Goebbels turned and walked back to the door. Outside stood the few remaining hard core of the faithful. They stood in stony silence. Then Goebbels cried,

'The Fuehrer is dead! The heart of Germany has ceased to beat . . .'

Famous War Books in Fontana

Rommel   Desmond Young   *35p*
'As the life and adventures of a swashbuckler and superb leader of men, *Rommel* can hardly be too highly commended to the public.'   *Evening Standard*

The First and the Last   Adolf Galland   *30p*
The rise and fall of the Luftwaffe—by Germany's greatest fighter pilot. 'Some of his air-battles read almost as fast as the Messerschmitts he flew, and his staff-battle accounts give the clearest picture yet of how the Germans lost their war in the air.'   *Time Magazine*

Winged Dagger   Roy Farran   *30p*
The thrilling account of Captain Farran's amazing career in the Special Air Service during World War II. 'Strongly recommended.'   *Evening Standard*

Malta Convoy
Peter Shankland and Anthony Hunter   *30p*
The fantastic saga of the tanker *Ohio*. It tells of the men who sailed her and also of the ship herself, who, broken-backed and sinking, carried not only the oil, Malta's sole hope of survival, but, the fate of the war itself.

Ten Thousand Eyes   Richard Collier   *30p*
The incredible exploits of the French Underground. 'A magnificent story, splendidly told.'   *Evening News*

Underwater Saboteur   Max Manus   *30p*
The thrilling story of Max Manus and his tiny band of Norwegian underground fighters in World War II, who crippled German shipping against enormous odds.

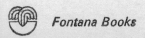

Fontana Books

Famous War Books in Fontana

Bridge on the River Kwai   Pierre Boulle   *25p*
One of the finest war novels ever written—the famous story of three remarkable men: *Col. Nicholson*, who was prepared to sacrifice everything—except his dignity; *Major Warden*, a modest hero and deadly killer; and *Cdr. Shears*, a man who escaped from hell and was ordered back.

Reach for the Sky   Paul Brickhill   *35p*
The unforgettable story of Douglas Bader, legless fighter pilot of World War II. 'This is a handbook of heroism . . . there is no medal yet for courage such as his.' *The People.* 'Moving and enthralling.' *Evening Standard*

Carve Her Name with Pride   R. J. Minney   *30p*
The story of Violette Szabo—wartime Secret Agent who, in solitary confinement, suffered atrocious tortures, but never gave away any of her secrets to the enemy. 'She was the bravest of us all.'   *Odette Churchill*

The Phantom Major   Virginia Cowles   *30p*
The astonishing exploits of David Stirling—commando hero of the desert war. 'An inspiring adventure story—the S.A.S. exploits were so fantastically daring that they can hardly fail to make exciting reading.'   *The Times*

Sinister Twilight   Noel Barber   *35p*
'We may never have a better book about the fall of Singapore.' *Sunday Mirror.* 'An entirely fresh light on what was regarded as a scandalous betrayal . . . so freshly and readably different.' *Evening News*

The War of the Running Dogs   Noel Barber   *40p*
A vivid, comprehensive book about the British defeat of the Malayan Communist guerrillas. 'Exciting and engrossing . . . a superlative slice of lucid, living history.'   *Sunday Express*

Fontana Books

Famous War Books in Fontana

The Tunnel Eric Williams *30p*
The story of the author's two dramatic escapes from prisoner-of-war camps that were unable to hold him. 'The atmosphere of prison-camp life is made more vivid than anything that one has read before. The excitement is maintained to the end.'
Glasgow Herald

The Wooden Horse Eric Williams *30p*
'An unusually good and gripping tale of a clever and courageous break from captivity and a nightmarish journey to freedom.' *The Observer*. 'It may be said with confidence that nothing better of its kind is likely to emerge from the Second World War . . . An amazing story.' *Glasgow Herald*

The Escapers Eric Williams *30p*
Breathtaking epics of escape collected by World War II's boldest escaper. 'Must surely represent the cream of escape literature. All his episodes are well chosen . . . They are long enough to be satisfying, and particularly, to give us a glimpse of the writer's character.' *The Listener*

More Escapers Eric Williams *30p*
'Few authors have written more vividly about wartime escapes than Eric Williams. In *More Escapers* he widens his scope to include peace-time escapologists.' *Coventry Evening Telegraph*. 'The reader is likely to find each of these escapes more enthralling than the last.' *Times Literary Supplement*

Send Down a Dove Charles MacHardy *35p*
'The finest submarine story to come out of either World War.' *Alistair MacLean*. A British sub in the closing years of World War II fights off mines, the Germans, and a mutiny below decks.

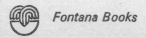 *Fontana Books*

Fontana Books

Fontana is best known as one of the leading paperback publishers of popular fiction and non-fiction. It also includes an outstanding, and expanding section of books on history, natural history, religion and social sciences.

Most of the fiction authors need no introduction. They include Agatha Christie, Hammond Innes, Alistair MacLean, Catherine Gaskin, Victoria Holt and Lucy Walker. Desmond Bagley and Maureen Peters are among the relative newcomers.

The non-fiction list features a superb collection of animal books by such favourites as Gerald Durrell and Joy Adamson.

All Fontana books are available at your bookshop or newsagent; or can be ordered direct. Just fill in the form below and list the titles you want.

-- -- -- -- -- -- -- -- -- -- -- -- -- -- -- --

FONTANA BOOKS, Cash Sales Department, P.O. Box 4, Godalming, Surrey. Please send purchase price plus 5p postage per book by cheque, postal or money order. No currency.

NAME (Block letters)

ADDRESS